I0720275

She wrote the fantasy. He became it.

TRIPLE XMAS

new york times bestselling author

ja huss

STORY FODDER
TRIPLE
XMAS
BOOK ONE

ABOUT THE BOOK

ScarletSins

Check here if you agree to be spanked. Hell yes.

Check here if you agree to CNC. Hell no.

This is my life. 100 questions about my most intimate fantasies, then a checklist about which of them I'll agree to.

Why am I doing this?

Why the hell do you think?

Money.

I need it.

The Seventy-Fifth Annual Triple Xmas Auction starts in three hours and I've got a price on my head.

Let's f-ing go.

Watcher

Check here if you've been watching her. For months.

Check here if you rigged the auction. Obviously.

This girl is my obsession. I know every word she's written.

Every fantasy she's afraid to live. Every desperate choice that led her here.

Why am I doing this?

Because she's mine.

She just doesn't know it yet.

The Seventy-Fifth Annual Triple Xmas Auction starts in three hours and I've already won.

Let the games begin.

A dark Christmas romance where the monster gets the girl.

TRIGGER WARNINGS FOR TRIPLE XMAS
A Guide for the Delightfully Unhinged

THE NAUGHTY LIST

Obsessive Hero
He Reads Her Books
She's Mine
Touch Her and Find Out
Pitch Black MMC
Predator/Prey
Forced Proximity
She Can't Leave
Claimed by a Billionaire
The Chase
Age Gap
Power Imbalance
Instant Obsession
Did I Mention Pitch Black?

CHAPTER 1
CALEB

Those who play in shadows always underestimate the light.

They think darkness is their ally, their shield against consequence.

They're wrong.

Darkness is just a temporary veil.

Nothing stays hidden forever.

Justice finds a way.

It always does.

You can run from it, hide from it, pay lawyers to build walls around it, but eventually it seeps through the cracks like light under a door.

Relentless. Patient. Inevitable.

And when you skirt around it for too long, when you think you've outsmarted the system, outmaneuvered the consequences, the only way it ends is… *messy.*

Violently messy, if I'm involved.

The kind of messy that comes with unmarked graves, desperate phone calls in the dead of night, and bloody clothes that need burning.

Every choice leaves a mark.

Every mark has a weight.

Every weight must be balanced.

I am the scales.

Justice isn't blind. That's a lie they tell children.

Justice has cold, calculating, patient eyes that watch, and wait, and remember everything.

If you earn it, you pay.

Blood for Blood hammers through my speakers as I navigate the icy switchback mountain road. *Fuck you, and fuck society too.* It's a roaring anthem that calms me after balancing the debts.

A ritual now.

A signal that the score has been evened.

An indicator of finality.

Justice done, I put the night's work behind me and concentrate on my next target—Scarletta Mae Desmond.

Erotica writer. DarkDesires Forum pen name, ScarletSins.

Lonely twenty-something with dirty blonde hair and hazel eyes that hide behind a computer screen.

No job worth mentioning—just freelance copywriting she's too distracted to finish.

No purpose beyond the stories she writes in the dark hours between midnight and dawn.

No ambition beyond the next chapter, the next comment, the next anonymous validation from strangers who don't know her name.

Unless you count her predictable cycle—words on the page, fingers between her legs—as ambition.

Which, knowing what I know about her, might be the most honest thing she does.

She thinks she's invisible. Thinks her online anonymity keeps her safe.

She's wrong.

I've been watching for months.

Learning her patterns. Her routines. The precise rhythm of her isolation.

And soon, very soon, she'll understand exactly what it means to be seen.

Completely.

Unavoidably.

Mine.

My driveway entrance sits under a ranch archway marked with a skull and crossbones instead of a cattle brand. I navigate the ice, driving slowly as I travel through an encroaching tunnel of hundred-year-old blue spruce.

For a moment, there is no sky above—just tree limbs. It's disorienting, something out of a dark fairy tale. But it never lasts, never long enough. Because a moment later the amber glow appears behind the floor-to-ceiling windows of my log estate.

The temperature on the dash reads twelve degrees. As I pull the Jeep around the side of the house toward the barn, I catch a glimpse of the hot tub on the back patio, its surface rolling with steam that rises like ghosts in the frigid air. The water glows an otherworldly red from the submerged lights, a beacon of heat in the frozen darkness.

The contrast is stark—civilized warmth against the brutal cold that wants to kill everything it touches.

I guide the vehicle into the barn's wide, dark mouth, the headlights sweeping across the interior before I drive fully inside. The structure swallows the Jeep whole, wood beams overhead and the lingering scent of hay and horse leather from the previous owners.

When I kill the engine, the hardcore Blood for Blood song becomes instant silence. The engine ticks as I look down at myself, studying the scarlet stains on my shirt, my pants, my arms, my hands.

I get out of the Jeep, walk over to the wood-burning furnace, and open the door. The embers glow bright orange under gray ash. The furnace in the horse barn is a nice touch. Part of the reason I bought this place six months ago.

After stoking the fire and loading it with logs, the flames rise up, fervent and yellow.

I strip out of my bloody clothes and feed them into the fire. The flames eat the fabric, racing along the threads until they are nothing but fire itself.

There is nothing about the past to dwell on.

Properly tuned minds only concentrate on the future.

Creating it. Manifesting it into being with planning, and recon, and proper execution.

So once the fabric is ash, I turn back to the open barn door and walk naked into the snow.

It crunches under my bare feet. Cold bites my calves, my thighs, my balls. I don't speed up. Don't hunch my shoulders or protect myself from the wind cutting across the property.

My skin prickles, then burns. But not enough to distract me from what comes next.

The invitation will arrive tonight. Tomorrow, on Christmas Eve, she will walk through my door believing she chose this. Believing the auction was chance, not orchestration. Believing I'm a stranger who won her fairly instead of the man who's been inside her apartment, her laptop, her head for six months.

My cock thickens as I cross the patio. Half-hard already and I haven't even touched myself, haven't thought about anything except logistics and cleanup for the past fourteen hours.

But now it's all about the future.

All about *her*.

The hot tub waits for me on the back deck, steam rising off the surface like mist on a hot, wet road. I step to the edge and look down at the churning water, lit up red from below.

Scarlet.

Scarletta.

I step into the water. It's scalding. The heat coats the cold chill as I sink down. When the water reaches my collarbone, I close my eyes.

Silence. Steam.

My cock is fully hard now.

I wrap my hand around it. The groan comes unbidden as I start stroking, slow and deliberate. Then I reach for the remote. I press the button, and the feed appears on the hundred-and-fifty-inch screen on the other side of the floor-to-ceiling windows.

And there she is.

My current obsession.

ScarletSins.

In this edit, she's typing. Furiously. Hair unwashed for two days, clothes rumpled, hasn't eaten since the day before. I've got a split screen going. One side from her webcam—looking directly at her face. the other side, her document, watching every single keystroke.

My pulse throbs in my cock, demanding and insistent.

The story she's writing in this cut is called "Prey."

It's a hybrid piece. Part *The Shining*—hedge maze in a blizzard, heroine running from something she can't name. Part *Meet Me in the Dark*—damaged man trying to un-fuck a mind-fucked woman who doesn't trust salvation. Part Apollo and Daphne mythology—get back here, you beautiful fucking victim.

She has no idea that I read every word before she posts it. That her laptop connects to my server the moment she opens it up. That I see her corrections, her deletions, her moments of doubt when she highlights entire paragraphs and hovers over the delete key before changing her mind.

Prey was released last month. I watched her type every fucking sentence. This is my favorite part here…

His hand closes around my throat from behind. I don't scream. Can't. The maze walls press in on both sides, snow falling so thick I can't see three feet ahead. "Did you think you could run from me?"

His voice is calm. Reasonable. Like I'm the irrational one for trying. "Did you really think I'd let you go?"

I claw at his wrist. He doesn't flinch.

"You're mine," he says against my ear. "You were mine the moment you walked into that room. The moment you signed your name. The moment you decided your body was worth selling."

My pulse throbs against his palm. He can feel it. I know he can.

"Please," I whisper.

"Please what?" His thumb presses into my jugular. Not enough to cut off air. Just enough to remind me he could. "Please stop? Please let you go? Or please fuck you right here in the snow until you forget you ever wanted to leave?"

She writes this shit because she needs it. Not wants —*needs*. The same way I need to cancel the darkness with the light of blood, she needs to be owned by something bigger than her small, suffocating life.

The stories aren't fiction. They're blueprints. Architectural renderings of her psyche laid bare in first-person present tense because that's how she experiences her own desperation —immediate, inescapable, happening *now*.

Every dominant in her stories sees through the protagonist's walls. Every one of them stalks, claims, corners, traps. Every single fucking one refuses to let her run.

And she comes back to this trope again and again.

Hedge mazes.

Basements.

Isolated cabins.

Locked rooms.

Scenarios where escape is impossible and surrender is inevitable.

My cock throbs in my fist. It's intoxicating, this spying I do. Watching her type words I've already memorized.

She craves the experience. Writes it because she can't have it. Can't trust herself to seek it out after every disappointment taught her that real men are nothing like the monsters in her head.

But I am.

I'm exactly like them.

Better, actually. Because I have resources.

Planning.

Six months of surveillance footage and behavioral pattern analysis.

I know her triggers, her limits, her tells when she's lying to herself.

She has no idea that every fantasy she's ever written is about to come true.

No idea that "Prey" isn't fiction—it's prophecy.

Christmas Eve is less than an hour away.

Then she's mine.

I stand. Water sluices off my shoulders, my chest, runs down my thighs. My hard cock juts out, unapologetic. I don't reach for the towel hanging on the deck rail, I just walk inside dripping.

The hardwood is cold under my bare feet. Water pools with each step, trailing behind me through the mudroom, the kitchen, down the hallway. My cock bobs with the movement, still hard and wanting.

The shower is hot enough to hurt. Water hammers my shoulders, my neck, runs down my chest and legs in rivers that pool at my feet before disappearing down the drain.

I scrub under my fingernails with the brush to get rid of the blood.

When I'm done, I shut off the water and dry efficiently. Gray sweatpants. Nothing else.

The whiskey bottle sits on the kitchen counter where I left it this morning. I pour two fingers neat, take it to the leather couch, set my laptop on the coffee table, and sit.

Even though the cut on the screen above the massive stone fireplace is still repeating, showing Scarletta as she furiously types out her deepest, darkest fantasies, that's not what I'm thinking about.

I've got new chapters to read.

The anticipation I feel before opening my laptop is pure arousal. Twenty-seconds later, the DarkDesires forum is loading.

Her profile appears first in my bookmarks. ScarletSins. Last active: 4 minutes ago.

This realization sparks abject lust. My cock throbs, interested now in a way I can't refuse it. My hand slides down into my sweats, gripping my shaft with intent.

Almost every night little Scarletta posts between 2,000 and 3,000 words. Always a full scene. Always filled with her most private, filthy desires.

The throbbing between my legs intensifies when I see the little green dot. When I realize she's online right now. This very fucking moment. Probably curled up in that pathetic blanket fort, laptop heating her thighs, coffee going cold beside her as her fingers work between her legs.

She masturbates two, sometimes three times a day.

I click her latest chapter.

The chapter is called *Confession*, the book is called *See Me, Spank Me, Cure Me*.

I read the opening line.

He has me on my knees with my wrists cuffed behind my back, and I've never felt more seen in my life.

My cock jerks in my palm.

She writes the scene like she's living it. First person, present tense, immediate. The protagonist—always some version of herself, always pretending she's not—kneels naked in front of a man who knows exactly what she needs before she does.

The dom in her story circles her slowly. Studying. I can see it perfectly because I've done this exact choreography in my head a thousand times with her body as the reference point.

"You're going to tell me what you want," he says. Not a question. A command.

"I can't," I whisper.

"You can. You will."

I stroke myself slowly, matching the rhythm of her words. She describes the way his hand tangles in her hair, forces her head back, makes her look at him. The vulnerability in that angle—throat exposed, eyes unable to hide.

"Tell me what you need," he says.

The words stick in my throat. Shame chokes them. But his grip tightens and I hear myself say it:

"I need you to use me."

"Be specific."

My grip tightens. I'm reading faster now, breathing harder.

"I need—" My voice breaks. *"I need your cock in my mouth. I need you to fuck my throat until I can't breathe. I need you to make me take it even when I gag."*

Jesus Christ.

He smiles. It's the most beautiful and terrifying thing I've ever seen.

"What else?"

"I need you to hurt me."

I nearly come as I work my cock in steady, deliberate strokes while my eyes devour each word she's written, every confession pouring directly from her psyche onto the screen in front of me.

This is her fantasy.

TPE. Throat fucking. Pain.

And tomorrow, I will make that fantasy come true.

I will have her down on her knees, gagging.

And she will come for me like the good little slut she is.

CHAPTER 2
SCARLETTA

The cursor blinks on my screen. Forty-three thousand words into *See Me, Spank Me, Cure Me* and I'm right there with her, my protagonist, feeling the exact moment she realizes she can't run anymore.

His hand is on her throat—not squeezing, just there, just claiming—and she's about to say it, the words I've been building toward for sixteen chapters. The words that will break her open.

"I'm yours."

My fingers are flying. I'm not even thinking anymore, just channeling it, the way her resistance finally cracks, the way she lets him see—

Footsteps in the hallway.

Heavy. Deliberate.

I freeze mid-sentence, hands hovering over the keyboard like I've been caught doing something illegal. Which is stupid. I'm just writing. I'm always just writing. Nobody cares what I do in this apartment. Nobody even knows I'm here most of the time.

The silence after the footsteps is worse than the sound.

Reality slams back into me like waking up from

anesthesia. That horrible jarring sensation of, *oh God, where am, I what was I doing, who am I* except I know exactly who I am and that's the problem.

I'm not her. The brave one. The one who surrenders because she's strong enough to choose it.

I'm Scarletta Mae Desmond. Twenty-two. Alone. Wearing leggings I put on three days ago—or was it four?—and Daddy's old hoodie that smells like the coffee I spilled Tuesday morning. Or maybe Monday. Time does this thing when I write where it stops being linear and becomes this soup I'm swimming through.

My apartment is a shoebox. Studio. Four hundred square feet of pretending I have my life together. The door is open.

Shit.

When did I—

Oh. The mail. I went to check the mail. There was nothing but grocery store flyers and a credit card offer for someone who doesn't live here anymore. I came back and had this idea about the scene where he first collars her, the way the leather would feel against her throat, heavy and permanent and terrifying, and I just... started writing.

The door's been open for—

I check the clock. 11:47 PM.

I went to get the mail at 7:30.

Jesus Christ, Scarletta.

The hallway light buzzes like it's angry about existing. Fluorescent. Institutional. The same light that's been flickering for two months because the building manager doesn't care about anything that isn't an actual fire.

I should get up. I should close the door. I should—

Yellow envelope.

It's stuck to my door like a parking ticket. Like a scarlet letter. Like every bad thing that's ever been official, and terrible, and unavoidable.

My body moves without permission. That's how it feels

when panic takes over—like I'm watching myself from a distance, like I'm narrating my own life except I don't want this scene, I never wanted this scene.

The envelope is thick. I know what it is before I touch it.

Yellow envelopes never bring good news. They bring the things you've been pretending aren't real. The things you've been hiding from by staying inside your head, inside your stories, inside the fantasy that you can just not deal with it and it'll go away.

My fingers shake when I pull it down. The tape makes this horrible ripping sound, loud in the silent hallway, fully pulling me back to the reality that it's almost midnight.

I can't open it in the hallway.

I step back inside. Close the door. Lock it. Like that'll help. Like I can lock out reality.

My laptop is still open on the floor, my blanket fort glowing from the fairy lights inside.

The place where I live.

Where I actually live, not this apartment, but inside the words, inside the stories where everything makes sense, and people want each other, and being broken is something beautiful instead of something that makes you unlovable.

I open the envelope and pull out the stack of papers.

FINAL NOTICE screams from the top in red letters. Bold. Unavoidable. Like they knew someone like me would need it spelled out, because we're good at ignoring things, those of us who live inside our heads.

My stomach knows before my brain does. That drop. That freefall. Like an elevator with cut cables.

I'm holding my breath.

When did I start holding my breath?

The words swim. My eyes can't focus. I blink and blink and the numbers don't change.

Four thousand two hundred dollars.

That's not—

That can't be. My rent is only ten-fifty a month. Which is criminal. A fucking felony, if you ask me. But this is Idaho Falls. A pretty place. Breathtakingly beautiful, actually. The markup for rentals is astronomical.

My mother has been telling me to move somewhere cheaper—she lives in Kansas City with her 'new family'. But the thought of moving from Idaho Falls to Kansas City makes me want to cry.

So I stay.

And I suffer for it. The point is—in order to be four-thousand two hundred dollars late in rent means... I count the months in my head. September. October. November. December. Four months. I paid September. I know I paid September. Didn't I?

Every time I try to fill out an application I'd get a story idea and I'd tell myself just let me get this chapter done first and then it'd be three days later and I'd have fifteen thousand new words and no job.

Three days to vacate.

Vacate. Such a polite word for get the fuck out.

Eviction proceedings happened yesterday.

I didn't show. Obviously. I didn't even know it was happening.

I read the notice again. Some stupid desperate part of me hoping I misread, hoping it's a mistake, hoping the universe isn't actually this cruel.

Four thousand two hundred.

Not four hundred. Not forty-two. Not some number I could maybe scrape together by selling my laptop, or my daddy's typewriter, or my body on a street corner somewhere.

Four thousand. Two hundred. Dollars.

I don't even understand how this is possible. How could I be four months behind in rent? Surely, there were signs. I would've noticed.

Right, Scarletta. You left your fucking front door open for four hours before you noticed.

My lungs burn.

Oh. Still holding my breath.

I exhale. It comes out shaky. Pathetic. The sound of a girl who's been pretending she's fine and just got caught.

Three days.

I sink down onto the floor, legs giving out, then I crawl back into my blanket fort, my laptop still glowing with the scene I was writing.

The scene where she finally surrenders.

Where she finally admits what she wants.

Where he catches her, and keeps her, and makes her his.

Fiction.

All of it fiction.

Because I can't pay rent in story comments.

I can't trade the forty-seven stories I've posted on DarkDesires for a roof over my head.

I can't surrender to a dominant who'll take care of me because this isn't a fucking fantasy, this is real life, and in real life you get evicted.

In real life... *you fail.*

CHAPTER 3
SCARLETTA

"I am *so* fucked. I am cosmically, catastrophically, thoroughly fucked. I am fucked in ways that require new vocabulary. I am fucked in dimensions scientists haven't discovered yet. I am—"

Ding.

The laptop notification cuts through my rant with the precision of a scalpel.

Silence rushes in. Loud silence. The kind that makes you aware of your own breathing, your heartbeat, the way the radiator has stopped hissing just to listen to you make a fool of yourself.

I stare at the glowing laptop screen, covered in blankets inside my fort.

Probably spam. Probably someone asking if I take commissions. Or—worse—another reader wanting to know when I'll update "Claimed" because I've left them hanging for three weeks while my obsession over *See Me, Spank Me, Cure Me* played out.

I fish it out, and stare at the screen.

The notification banner shows a username I don't recognize: AuctionAdmin_DarkDesires

Ok.

I click it open.

SUBJECT: Exclusive Invitation - 75th Annual Triple Xmas Auction

Dear ScarletSins,

Based on your exceptional content and engagement on DarkDesires, you've been selected for an exclusive opportunity.

Would you wrap yourself up as the perfect gift for a generous benefactor this holiday season?

The Triple Xmas Auction connects willing participants with verified high-net-worth individuals seeking companionship for Christmas Eve, December 24th, through Christmas Day, December 25th.

Selection Process: Right Now

Christmas Eve Bidding: December 24th, 10:00 AM

Service Expectation: Starts immediately after auction, ends December 25th, 12:00 PM

Payment Disbursement: December 25th, 12:00 PM

Compensation:

Minimum guaranteed payout: $20,000

Performance bonuses available

All transactions confidential and legally binding.

Make this Christmas unforgettable—for yourself AND for someone who values exactly what you offer.

Interested? Click below to review terms and begin the selection process.

[CONFIRM INTEREST]

I read it twice. Three times. Twenty thousand times. Once for each dollar. Minimum.

My hands are shaking.

This is insane. This is—this has to be a scam. Or trafficking. Or some elaborate phishing scheme designed specifically for broke erotica writers with eviction notices.

But.

Twenty thousand dollars.

The number blazes in my mind like a neon sign. Twenty thousand. Two-zero-zero-zero-zero.

Twenty-four-ish hours.

Christmas Eve at ten AM through Christmas Day at noon.

My brain starts mathing, defensive and desperate all at once. If I was going anywhere except my usual blanket fort of seasonal depression, I could technically still make it back in time for... what? Presents? Family dinner?

I mentally catalog my pathetic excuse for Christmas plans: me, my laptop, leftover ramen if I'm lucky, and the crushing silence of being completely alone while the rest of the world pretends to be jolly.

I'm not going anywhere on Christmas. There's nowhere to go, no one waiting, no tree with my name on a single wrapped package underneath it. But the point is—and this feels important somehow, like my brain is grasping for any rationalization it can find—the point is that I *could*. If I had somewhere to be, this wouldn't even interfere.

It's... considerate? Is that the word? Weirdly thoughtful for what is clearly, obviously, definitely—

Auction.

The word sits in my brain like a stone.

Auction. Like... sex... auction?

That can't be right. Can it? Is that what this is?

My hands are trembling so badly I nearly drop my laptop as I push it up to my nose like I'm checking for fine print, or hidden messages, or some kind of "GOTCHA, you idiot" disclaimer.

I read the whole thing one more time. Every word. Every implication.

Make this Christmas unforgettable—for yourself AND for someone who values exactly what you offer.

It *is* a sex auction.

It's an actual, literal, what-the-fuck-is-my-life sex auction, and they're inviting me.

Why?

I mean... okay. Yes. I'm a good writer. My erotica stories have game—twelve thousand followers don't lie, and "Owned" hit the top of the Psychological Dark Romance leaderboard for six consecutive weeks. My readers say things like "most realistic D/s dynamics I've ever read" and "how does she know what it feels like?" and I sit there behind my screen, anonymous and invisible, glowing with validation I can't get anywhere else.

But that's words. That's fiction. That's me, alone in my apartment at 3 AM, pouring every filthy fantasy I'll never actually live into characters who are braver, and prettier, and far more fuckable than I could ever be.

I look down at myself.

Yuk.

Who the fuck would bid on this?

The forum dings again—a sharp, invasive sound that makes me flinch.

[CONFIRM INTEREST]

And below it, in cold, unforgiving red numbers:

Invitation expires in: 0:59

0:58

0:57

A minute? I'm supposed to decide my entire fate—whether to potentially sell myself to a stranger for Christmas—in one fucking minute?

No.

No way.

Absolutely not. This is exactly how stupid, desperate young women end up as the cautionary-tale protagonist in someone else's erotica story—the kind where things start off intriguing, and flattering, and just a little dangerous, and then three chapters in she's locked in a basement wearing a dog collar while her family files a missing person's report that goes nowhere because she signed a fucking contract.

I know how these stories go. I've written these stories.

The difference is, my protagonists always get their happy ending. They're always secretly brilliant and unexpectedly beautiful beneath their mousy exterior, and the dangerous man always turns out to have a heart of gold buried under all that trauma and control issues.

It's fantasy. It's fiction.

Real life doesn't work that way.

Real life is Derek laughing when I used my safeword. Real life is men who see vulnerability and think target. Real life is me, four months behind on rent, scrolling through an invitation to what is very clearly an illegal sex trafficking operation disguised as a "private event," and actually—God help me—actually considering it because twenty thousand dollars would solve every single problem in my pathetic existence.

0:51

0:50

My phone rings.

I swear my heart skips—no, lurches—forward in my chest, slamming against my ribs like it's trying to escape through bone and tissue. Seventeen beats condensed into one violent thud that leaves me breathless and dizzy.

I drop the laptop. It tumbles gracelessly into the pillow mound beside me.

Then I'm scrambling. Limbs tangling in blankets. Hands patting frantically through the fabric chaos of my blanket fort.

Where the fuck did I put it? Where—

There. Wedged between two cushions, vibrating insistently.

I yank it free.

The screen glows up at me, bright and merciless in the dim string-light glow of my apartment.

The caller ID mocks me. Mocks every single one of my pessimistic, cautionary, sensible thoughts from three seconds ago.

Because the name displayed in crisp white letters is:

AuctionAdmin_DarkDesires

I laugh.

It bursts out of me—high-pitched, disbelieving, borderline hysterical. The kind of laugh that would make a therapist lean forward with concern and scribble notes about "inappropriate affect" and "dissociative response to stress."

And in my panic-stricken, laugh-strangled fumbling, my thumb slips.

Slides right across the green "accept call" button.

Is it a slip though, Scarletta? Is it?

"Fuck—"

"Scarletta?"

The voice that emerges from my phone speaker is male. Deep. Cultured. The kind of smooth baritone that belongs to someone who's never had to raise his voice to be obeyed. Professional yet somehow intimate, like he's speaking directly into my ear instead of through cellular towers and digital compression.

My stomach drops straight through the blankets, through the floor, through four stories of modern, walk-up, soul-less apartment building, into the frozen December earth below.

Shit.

"Um... yeah?" My voice comes out small. Uncertain. Like I'm a child caught stealing cookies, not a twenty-two-year-old woman who accidentally-on-purpose-maybe answered her phone.

"Good evening." There's warmth there. Genuine pleasure, maybe, or an excellent facsimile. "I hope your writing is going well. I'm such a fan of your work."

My brain stutters to a halt.

He knows. Whoever this is—this stranger calling from the DarkDesires admin account at nearly midnight on Christmas Eve Eve—he knows I write. He's read my stories. He's... a fan?

The cognitive dissonance makes my head spin.

"I'm sorry..." I press my free hand against my forehead, trying to ground myself in something real. The pressure of skin on skin. The slight dampness of nervous sweat. "Who are you?"

"I'm the one who just sent you the message." His tone shifts slightly. Still pleasant, but there's an edge now. Purpose. Like a salesman moving in for the close. "I don't want to pressure you, but I'm sure you've noticed the countdown timer. And I really do need an answer soon."

The countdown.

Right.

The fucking countdown that's currently at—I glance at my laptop screen—thirty-three seconds and dropping.

Something in my chest constricts. Not panic exactly. Something worse. The terrible, seductive pull of… *what if*.

But no.

No.

This is insane. This is dangerous. This is every true crime podcast I've ever listened to condensed into one phone call.

"Right. The countdown." I force steel into my voice. The kind of firmness I've never managed in real life but can conjure in fiction without effort. "Listen, I'm a no. OK? So… I don't know what this is, but… yeah. No. Hard pass. Thanks but no thanks."

I jab the red "end call" button before I can do something phenomenally stupid.

Like say yes.

Like ask questions.

Like let that smooth, confident voice talk me into believing this could possibly be anything other than a setup for disaster.

My hand is shaking. The phone trembles in my grip, screen going dark, and I have exactly three seconds of relief before it lights up again.

AuctionAdmin_DarkDesires.

Of course.

I don't answer. I just stare at the screen, watching it ring. Once. Twice. Three times. Four.

Then the call stops.

The silence feels worse somehow.

This is stupid. This isn't real. Shit like this doesn't happen —not to people like me, not in actual reality. It's a fantasy. A dark, fucked-up fantasy that belongs in fiction where it's safe, and contained, and can't actually hurt anyone.

A notification dings from my laptop.

I'm scrambling again before I consciously decide to move. Hands diving back into the pillow mound, shoving blankets aside with increasing desperation to get to my computer, then I yank it into my lap.

The notification is coming from a tab I opened several minutes ago—the one I pulled up in a fit of masochistic curiosity to confirm that yes, I really do only have forty-seven dollars and thirty-two cents to my name.

Except I should be logged out—they do that for you. Automatically. When you leave your bank account wide open in a tab. Because God knows, Scarletta, and other morons just like her, can't possibly be expected to log out of something as mundane as an account holding her entire net worth.

But I'm not logged out. And on screen is some kind of receipt. A transaction record. I squint at the small text, trying to make sense of what I'm seeing in the dim glow of string lights.

Is that my...

Holy shit.

It's my account balance.

But it can't be my account balance.

Because I have forty-seven dollars. Not one thousand and forty-seven dollars. Not a randomly round deposit of exactly one thousand dollars that appeared in my checking account at 11:59 PM on December 23th with a transaction note that reads simply:

Good faith deposit
AuctionAdmin_DarkDesires.

I refresh the page.

The number doesn't change.

One thousand and forty-seven dollars.

The number stares back at me, impossible and real.

Another ding.

A new notification banner appears at the top of my screen, overlaying the bank website with a message from DarkDesires PM's:

> Good faith deposit. It's yours regardless of your decision. All you have to do is click [CONFIRM INTEREST] to proceed.

Five seconds.
Four.
Three.
I click confirm.

CHAPTER 4
SCARLETTA

The screen blinks.

Then goes black.

No. No no no no—

What did I just do?

My heart slams forward, a reminder that I'm an idiot. A complete fucking idiot. Because that's what happens when you click random links from anonymous strangers who somehow have your phone number, and your bank account information, and your name—

This is a phishing scheme.

Obviously.

It's always a phishing scheme. Or malware. Or—what are they called? Trojan horses? Are those still a thing? Do people still use that terminology or did I just age myself by referencing a term from third grade?

God, I'm so stupid.

So monumentally, catastrophically stupid.

The kind of stupid that gets featured on true crime podcasts where the host uses that particular tone of sympathetic condescension while describing the victim's poor choices. "Scarletta Mae Desmond, 22, clicked a suspicious link at 11:59 PM on Christmas Eve Eve. Her dismembered body was discovered three days later in a storage unit in Newark."

My laptop is still black.

Completely dark.

I stare at the void of the screen, my own pale reflection visible in the glossy surface. Wide eyes. Messy hair pulled into a bun that's mostly fallen apart. The string lights behind me casting an amber glow that makes me look jaundiced.

I look like someone who makes terrible decisions.

Because I am someone who makes terrible decisions.

This is why I don't have friends. This is why Derek left. This is why my mother stopped calling. Because I'm fundamentally broken in ways that make me unsuited for actual human interaction. I should just stay in my blanket fort forever, writing about people who are braver than me, smarter than me, better at—

The screen blinks.

It's not black anymore.

There's... something loading. A progress bar. White text on a dark background that looks nothing like my normal desktop.

Initializing secure download...

TOR Browser Installation Package

Timer:

00:59

00:58

Another countdown.

Another impossible choice with no time to think.

Am I really this stupid? Am I actually going to—

A notification dings.

DarkDesires forum. Still open in another tab somehow, which shouldn't be possible if my computer just got hijacked, but clearly the rules of logic don't apply tonight.

The message is from AuctionAdmin_DarkDesires:

> You have $1000 good faith money. The link is safe. TOR is a secure browser used for anonymous communication. Look it up. You have 45 seconds.
>
> Look it up.

Right.

Because I definitely have time to research internet security protocols while a countdown timer ticks away and my entire computer is potentially being compromised by—

My fingers are already moving.

Open Chrome. New tab. Google search. "What is TOR browser."

The results populate immediately. Wikipedia. Reddit threads. A dozen tech articles with varying levels of paranoia.

The Onion Router (TOR) is free and open-source software for enabling anonymous communication...

...used by journalists, activists, and individuals seeking privacy...

...not inherently dangerous, though often associated with the dark web...

I skim faster, absorbing fragments. It's legitimate. It's actually a real thing. Not a virus. Not malware. Just a browser that lets you access parts of the internet that aren't indexed by Google.

The parts where illegal things happen.

The parts where people get trafficked.

My stomach twists.

But also... the parts where people maintain privacy. Where

whistleblowers operate. Where, apparently, sex auctions that pay twenty thousand dollars for twenty-four hours exist.

The timer on the download page reads twelve seconds.

I click download.

The progress bar fills. Fast. Faster than it should for something that's supposedly complex and secure. Maybe that's how you know it's legitimate? Or maybe that's how you know you're being scammed?

I don't know.

I don't know anything except that I'm already in too deep to back out now.

The installation completes. A new icon appears on my desktop—an onion. Cute. Very on-the-nose for something called The Onion Router.

My laptop screen blinks again. Dings.

I actually whimper.

How many times can I be this stupid? How many red flags do I need before my brain engages and I do the smart thing and shut this entire operation down?

DarkDesires forum. Another message from AuctionAdmin_DarkDesires.

This one contains a link. Long. Incomprehensible. A string of random letters and numbers ending in .onion.

The next message appears before I can spiral further.

> Double click the onion icon. Copy the link I sent you. Paste it into the address bar at the top. Press enter.

I stare at the instructions.

That's it.

That's the whole thing.

Double click. Copy. Paste. Enter.

Instructions written like I'm five years old. Like I've never used a computer before. Like I need someone to hold my hand through the most basic possible task that literally everyone on the internet knows how to—

Oh god.

I do need someone to hold my hand.

Because I'm sitting here staring at these four simple steps like they're written in a foreign language, my brain completely offline, panic making everything feel slow, and thick, and wrong.

It's just copy pasta. Everyone does this. You've done this a thousand times. Just... do the thing.

My hands are shaking.

I double click the onion icon.

The browser opens. It looks... normal. Weirdly normal. Just a plain window with an address bar and some basic navigation buttons. No scary warnings. No red flags. Nothing to indicate I've just opened a portal to the criminal underworld where my identity will be stolen, and my bank account drained, and my soul harvested for—

Stop. Breathe. Copy the link.

I switch back to DarkDesires. Highlight the incomprehensible string of letters and numbers ending in .onion. Right click. Copy.

My heart is pounding so hard I can feel it in my throat.

This is fine. This is normal. You're just clicking things. Nothing bad has happened yet.

Yet.

I switch back to the TOR browser. Click in the address bar. Right click. Paste.

The link appears. Long and meaningless and definitely leading somewhere I shouldn't go.

My cursor hovers over the enter key.

Don't do this. You still have time. You can close the browser. Delete everything. Pretend this never happened. The thousand dollars is already in your account—they said you could keep it regardless. Just walk away.

But I won't walk away.

I know I won't.

Because I'm already calculating. One thousand dollars buys me... what? Two weeks? Maybe three if I eat nothing but ramen? It doesn't cover the eviction that's happening in three days. Doesn't stop the inevitable. Doesn't fix anything.

But *twenty* thousand dollars...

I press enter.

The screen goes white.

Then an image loads.

Mountains.

Snow-covered peaks against a pale winter sky. The photograph is beautiful in that crisp, almost painful way that makes you feel the cold just looking at it. Professional quality. The kind of landscape that belongs on a calendar or a screensaver.

There's nothing else.

Just mountains and snow and a single text box centered in the middle of the screen with a label above it that reads:

Access Code

I wait.

Nothing happens.

No pop-ups. No warnings. No instructions. Just mountains and an empty box and the sick feeling in my stomach that I've just done something monumentally stupid and there's no going back.

Ding.

The forum notification makes me jump.

Another message from AuctionAdmin_DarkDesires.

This one contains a single line of text: a string of twelve characters. Letters and numbers. No explanation.

The access code.

Obviously.

Because they're still holding my hand. Still walking me

through this like I'm a child who can't figure anything out on her own.

You can't, whispers the part of my brain that sounds suspiciously like Derek. *You're exactly as incompetent as you think you are.*

I copy the access code.

Paste it into the text box.

My finger hovers over the enter key again.

Last chance. This is your last chance to stop being stupid.

I press enter.

The screen blinks.

For one horrible second I think it's going to go black again, that this whole thing is just an elaborate loop designed to fuck with me, to prove that I'm gullible, and desperate, and—

A web portal loads.

It's simple. Clean. Almost clinical in its design. White background. Black text. No branding. No logos. Just a header at the top that reads:

Triple Xmas Auction

Confidential Participant Agreement

Below that, a single line:

Logged in as: Access Code 847-SK-2847

Not my name.

Just a code.

Anonymous.

That should make me feel better. It doesn't.

Because beneath the login confirmation is a form. Multiple pages, judging by the scroll bar on the right side. Fields and checkboxes and sections with headers like Physical Description, and Limits And Boundaries, and Medical History.

At the very bottom, a note in smaller text:

This form requires approximately 3 hours to complete.

Three *hours*?

Three hours of my life to fill out a form that will determine whether some anonymous stranger pays twenty thousand dollars to... what?

Fuck me?

Own me?

Use me for twenty-four hours in ways I can't even fully imagine?

This is when I notice there's another timer. They are not fucking around about the three hours.

It's already counting down...

CHAPTER 5
SCARLETTA

The form is organized into sections with clinical precision. Each one more invasive than the last.

Part I: Psychological Profile

Answer all questions honestly and completely. Your responses will be shared with potential buyers to ensure compatible matching.

My stomach drops.

Shared with buyers. Plural.

Which means multiple people will read whatever I write here. Multiple strangers will know things about me I've never told anyone. Things I barely admit to myself.

You write about this stuff online, I remind myself. Thousands of people have read your darkest fantasies.

But that's different. Those are stories. Fiction. Characters who aren't me.

This is... this *is* me.

Question 1: Describe your darkest sexual fantasy in detail. What about it arouses you?

I stare at the text box. Cursor blinking. Waiting.

The smart thing would be to lie. Give them something generic. Something that doesn't expose the twisted parts of my brain.

But they're paying me twenty thousand dollars minimum. They want honesty.

And maybe—maybe I want someone to finally know.

I start typing.

I read it back.

Delete it.

Retype almost the exact same thing.

Delete it again.

Just fucking write it. They already have your bank account information. What's a little soul-baring compared to that?

I type it a third time and force myself to move on before I can second-guess.

Question 2: What is your relationship with shame regarding your sexual desires?

Oh, we're just diving right into the deep end, aren't we?

Question 3: Have you ever wanted to be watched without your knowledge or permission? Why does this appeal to you?

Question 4: Describe a time you felt most vulnerable during a sexual or intimate experience. What made it significant?

My vision blurs.

I'm not crying. I'm just tired.

Liar.

Question 5: What role does fear play in your arousal? Be specific.

Be specific. As if the general answer wouldn't be damning enough.

I'm a therapist's wet dream at this point.

Or nightmare. Probably nightmare.

Question 6: Have you ever fantasized about someone manipulating circumstances to get close to you? Describe this fantasy.

What the fuck kind of question—

I stare at it.

Read it again.

Someone manipulating circumstances.

This is either the most insightful psychological profiling I've ever seen, or whoever wrote this questionnaire has access to my brain.

Neither option is comforting.

Question 7: What is your experience level with BDSM practices? What have you tried? What have you only imagined?

Finally, a straightforward question.

Question 8: Describe your ideal dominant partner. What qualities matter most?

I could write a dissertation on this.

I write a paragraph instead. Essentially describing a fictional character. Because men like that don't exist in real life.

You're about to find out if they do.

Shut up, brain.

Question 9: What are you hoping to gain from this experience? Be honest.

They keep saying "be honest" like I might be tempted to lie.

I'm past lying at this point. I've already confessed to wanting to be manipulated and watched without consent. What's a little financial desperation on top of that?

There.

The pathetic truth in all its glory.

Question 10: What is your greatest fear about participating in this auction?

I almost laugh.

My greatest fear?

How much time do they have?

I hit enter before I can delete it.

The form advances to the next section.

Part II: Experience & Availability Menu
Select all activities you consent to during your contracted period.
Compensation is cumulative based on selections. All activities are
optional.

Holy shit, it's a menu.
A literal menu of sex acts with price tags attached.

Base Compensation (Mandatory): $20,000 ✓ Agreed

And below that, categories. Tiers. Like I'm ordering appetizers at a restaurant except the appetizers are various forms of sexual degradation.

Tier 1: Foundational Activities ($500 each)

The list includes things I've already tried. Things that seem almost quaint compared to what I've written about.
Light bondage. Spanking. Blindfolds. Orgasm control. Temperature play.
I check them all.
Five hundred dollars each.
That's... that's twenty-five hundred dollars for things I've fantasized about anyway.
You're selling yourself.
I'm selling my time. And my consent. Which is mine to sell.
The justification sounds hollow even in my own head.

847-Sk-2847 Tier 1 Total: $2,500

The number appears at the bottom of the section, updating automatically.
Twenty-two thousand five hundred total now.

Tier 2: Intermediate Activities ($1,000 Each)

This is where it gets more intense.

Heavy bondage. Moderate impact play—marks allowed, the description specifies, like someone might want proof afterward that this happened.

Complete sensory deprivation.

Objectification.

Total Power Exchange - 24 hours.

My cursor hovers over that last one.

All autonomy relinquished for contract duration.

That's what I want, isn't it? What I write about constantly? Complete surrender to someone who knows what to do with it?

I check the box.

And the others.

Because I'm already here. Already doing this. Might as well commit.

847-SK-2847 Tier 2 Total: $5,000

Twenty-seven thousand five hundred total.

Enough to pay off my eviction and have money left over for... what? First and last month's rent somewhere new? Food? Basic survival?

Keep going.

Tier 3: Advanced Activities ($2,500-$5,000 Each)

I read through the list.

Psychological dominance. Mind games. Gaslighting desires. Using participant's own fantasies/writing against them.

My breath catches.

Using participant's own fantasies/writing against them.

They know.

They know I write. They know I have a forum account. They know my darkest fantasies are documented in forty-seven stories for anyone to read.

And they're offering twenty-five hundred dollars for permission to weaponize that knowledge against me.

I check the box.

Forced confession. Verbalization of shameful desires under duress.

Check.

Mirror work. Forced observation of own submission.

Check.

I skip the severe impact play. The breath play. The knife play, needle play, and fire play.

There's a difference between fantasy and having someone actually put a knife to my skin, and I'm not ready to cross that line for any amount of money.

847-SK-2847 Tier 3 Total: $7,500

Thirty-five thousand total.

I'm shaking.

Tier 4: Extreme Activities ($10,000-$50,000 each)

Consensual non-consent.

Public humiliation.

Recording.

Sharing—multiple partners.

Extended captivity beyond twenty-four hours.

Permanent marking.

Watersports.

Scat play.

I don't check any of them.

Fifty thousand dollars for a rape fantasy means someone out there is willing to pay fifty thousand dollars for a rape fantasy, and that level of desire terrifies me more than the act itself.

847-SK-2847 Tier 4 Total: $0

Still thirty-five thousand.

Tier 5: Additional Considerations ($1,500-$3,000 each)

The list is longer here. More specific.

Exhibitionism—scenes performed in front of mirrors, windows, or buyer's observation. Fifteen hundred dollars to be watched.

I check it.

Verbal degradation. Name-calling. Humiliation through language.

Check.

Servitude. Domestic tasks while naked or restrained.

Check.

Sleep deprivation. Food control. Bathroom control.

I hesitate on bathroom control.

Permission required. Door open. Buyer may observe.

That's... that's humiliating in a way that has nothing to do with sex.

That's control over basic bodily functions.

That's reducing me to something less than human.

Fifteen hundred dollars.

I check the box.

I skip anal play, deep throat training, orgasm prohibition, but then…

Forced orgasms until unconsciousness?
I mean…
Check.

847-SK-2847 Tier 5 Total: $9,000

The grand total appears at the bottom of the screen.

Total Compensation: $44,000

Forty-four *thousand dollars.*
For twenty-four hours of complete surrender to a stranger who will have access to my psychological profile, my writing, my darkest fears and desires.
A stranger who will tie me up, and blindfold me, and control when I eat, and sleep, and piss.
Who will call me degrading names and make me confess things I've never said out loud.
Who will use my own words against me.
Who will make me watch myself in mirrors as I submit to everything I've only ever written about.
Who will make me come until I pass out.
Forty-four thousand dollars.
I can pay off my eviction. All my bills, gone. Instant new life. Get a new apartment. Something bigger. With an office, or at least a bedroom. Have a safety net while I figure shit out. Maybe even hire a cover designer and publish one of my stories for real on Amazon instead of DarkDesires Forum.
All I have to do is click submit.
My cursor hovers over the button.
This is insane. You're insane. You're going to get trafficked or murdered or—
The timer at the top of the screen shows seven minutes remaining.

Seven minutes to decide if I'm the kind of person who does this.

If I'm desperate enough.

Broken enough.

Brave enough.

You're none of those things. You're just scared, and alone, and out of options.

My finger hovers over the touchpad.

What would your mother say?

That question should stop me.

It doesn't.

Because my mother married a man she didn't love to avoid being alone in college. Then did it again after my daddy died. She's got stepsons now. Stepsons she treats far better than she ever did me.

It doesn't even bother me though. Her life sounds like Hell. She performed a version of herself for thirty years until she forgot who she really was.

She disappeared into safety and called it good.

I refuse to disappear.

Even if it means doing something reckless. Even if it means selling myself to a stranger. Even if it means confronting every fear and fantasy I've spent years hiding from.

At least I'll be *seen.*

I click submit.

The screen goes black.

For one horrible second I think the browser has crashed. That I've lost everything. That the whole thing was a scam and I've just confessed my darkest secrets to the void for nothing.

Or worse—that it was real and I just lost three hours of work and won't be able to fill the form out again in the six minutes I have left.

Then a message appears.

> Submission Received.

> Thank You, Participant 847-Sk-2847.

> Further Instructions Will Be Provided Shortly.

The timer disappears.

I sit back.

It's two-fifty-five in the morning now. I've been staring at this screen for three hours, excavating my psyche and assigning dollar values to my boundaries.

My phone vibrates.

I nearly jump out of my skin.

A text message. Unknown number.

> Take nothing with you but your phone and go downstairs to the lobby. A car is waiting.

I read it again.

Now?

Right now?

My apartment is a disaster. Dirty dishes, blanket fort catastrophe, and I'm wearing yoga pants and a t-shirt I've been in for two days. I haven't showered. Haven't brushed my teeth. Haven't—

My phone vibrates again.

> Now, Scarletta.

They know my name.

Of course they know my name. They have my bank account. My psychological profile. Forty-seven stories worth of my deepest fantasies.

They know everything.

Take nothing but your phone.

I stand on shaking legs.

Look around my apartment one last time.

The blanket fort. The laptop. The eviction notice on the floor.

One-thousand forty-seven dollars in my checking account.

Forty-four thousand waiting for me downstairs.

I pick up my phone and I leave.

CHAPTER 6
CALEB

There are many ways to be depraved.

Some people lack moral boundaries.

Some find pleasure in cruelty and pain.

And some, like my good little slut, Scarletta, twist desire into something dark and consuming.

She and I have that in common.

I'm in bed. Naked on top of the covers. Cock in hand.

The laptop sits on the nightstand, screen angled so I can see it clearly. Three feeds on the display. Top left: her apartment, wide shot from the camera hidden in her smoke detector. Top right: close-up from the webcam I activated six months ago. Bottom: keystroke logger, every letter she types appearing in real-time.

She's been filling out the questionnaire for nine minutes.

I've been hard since she clicked the link.

My stroke is slow. Controlled. I'm not rushing this. I want to savor every second of watching her confess what she needs.

What she needs from *me*.

The thousand dollars was a calculated risk. Not a bribe—insurance. Keep her focused. Keep her engaged. Make sure she didn't panic and close the browser before she got far enough in to see what she was really agreeing to.

Worth every penny when I watched her face change. When doubt, became curiosity, became arousal.

And the phone call.

My grip tightens.

Her voice. Breathy. Nervous.

That little hitch when she said, "Fuck," instead of *hello*.

She was scared, yes. But underneath she was interested. I heard it. The way she didn't hang up immediately. The way she listened.

She liked my voice.

Good.

She's going to hear it a lot over the next twenty-four hours.

The keystroke feed updates.

Question 1: Describe your darkest sexual fantasy in detail. What about it arouses you?

I stop stroking. Wait.

Her cursor blinks in the text box for thirty-seven seconds.

Then she starts typing.

Being held captive by someone who sees me completely—

I resume stroking. Slower now.

She wants captivity. Not rope and chains. Psychological captivity. The kind where escape is possible but surrender is inevitable.

She wants someone who's read everything she's written.

I have.

Every story. Every draft. Every deleted paragraph she wrote and reconsidered and cut because it was too honest.

—knows my fears and desires better than I do—

Better than she does.

That's what makes my cock throb. Not the captivity fantasy itself. The fact that she craves someone who understands her needs before she can articulate them.

Someone who sees through her walls and dismantles them piece by piece until she has nowhere left to hide.

She wants to be known.

Completely.

Darkness and all.

And desired *because* of it.

Not despite it.

I stroke faster.

This is why I chose her. This exact need. The desperation to be seen by someone intelligent enough to understand what she can't say out loud. Someone who won't flinch when he discovers how dark her desires run.

Someone who'll give her exactly what she's too ashamed to ask for.

I've been watching her for six months. I know her better than she knows herself.

And in—I glance at the countdown timer on screen—nine hours and forty-two minutes, I'm going to prove it to her.

Question 2: What is your relationship with shame regarding your sexual desires?

Her cursor blinks for ninety seconds this time.

Longer hesitation. More resistance.

Then she starts typing.

I read the first line and my cock jumps in my fist.

She's ashamed of what she wants.

Deeply ashamed.

Writes under a pseudonym because the humiliation of being discovered would destroy her. Her mother's voice still echoing in her skull—*nice girls don't think about that*—even though she knows intellectually it's bullshit.

But the shame doesn't stop the arousal.

It *feeds* it.

I stroke faster. My breathing goes shallow.

This is perfect.

This is exactly what I need.

She's aroused by dominance, control, fear, pain—all the things she thinks she shouldn't want. The shame sharpens the desire. Makes it forbidden. Makes it dangerous.

And she wants someone who won't judge her for it.

Someone who'll *make* her admit what she craves even when she's too mortified to speak.

I pause. Process that.

She doesn't just want acceptance.

She wants to be forced to confess.

Wants the decision taken from her. Wants someone to drag the truth out of her so she doesn't have to volunteer it. So she can tell herself it wasn't her fault. He *made* me say it.

My grip tightens.

I can work with this.

The shame is leverage. Psychological pressure I can apply precisely. Make her speak her desires aloud while she's blushing, trembling, hating herself for needing what I'm about to give her.

Question 3: Have you ever wanted to be watched without your knowledge or permission? Why does this appeal to you?

Her cursor doesn't blink this time.

She starts typing immediately.

I slow my stroke. Watch the words appear on the keystroke feed.

Yes.

One word. No hesitation.

Then she elaborates.

She fantasizes about being observed during her most private moments. When she's writing. Touching herself. Crying. Completely unguarded.

My hand stills on my cock.

She wants to be watched without knowing.

Wants someone studying her when she thinks she's alone. When the performance stops and the real Scarletta emerges—the one who writes depravity at three AM in unwashed clothes, who cries over rejection emails, who touches herself while reading comments on her own stories.

I've already done this.

I've watched her write every word. Seen her masturbate to fantasies she typed with the other hand. Witnessed her sob into her pillow after her mother ignored her birthday text.

And she wants this.

She *craves* it.

The violation and intimacy tangled together until they're inseparable.

I resume stroking. Faster now.

What makes my cock throb isn't just that she wants surveillance. It's *why*.

She performs for everyone. Edits herself. Hides. But alone, she's raw. Real. Authentic in ways she can never be when she knows someone's looking.

And she wants to be desired for *that* version.

The unguarded one.

The real one.

The one no one else gets to see.

She wants proof that her darkness doesn't repel. That being watched at her worst—her most vulnerable, her most depraved—makes someone want her *more*.

Not despite who she really is.

Because of it.

I stroke harder.

She doesn't know I've been watching.

Doesn't know I've seen every private moment.

Doesn't know I've catalogued her routines, her habits, her tells.

When I reveal it—and I will, eventually—she'll be horrified.

Violated.

Furious.

And so fucking wet she won't be able to stand.

Question 4: Describe a time you felt most vulnerable during a sexual or intimate experience. What made it significant?

I stop stroking completely.

My jaw clenches.

She's typing about the forum where she met another man. The fantasies she shared. How she trusted him with things she'd never told anyone.

How he violated her safeword.

Kept going while she begged him to stop.

Laughed at her. Called her *bad at this*. Then ghosted her like she was nothing.

I set my laptop aside. Stand. Walk to the window naked, cock still hard, mind clear.

Derek Morrison.

Twenty-four years old. IT consultant. Lived in Boise.

Lived.

Past tense.

I found him four months ago. Wasn't difficult. She'd mentioned enough details in old forum posts—before she learned to scrub her digital footprint. His username. The city. His job.

Took me three days to confirm his identity.

Two weeks to study his patterns.

One night to make him pay.

Taser to the neck. Forty-five seconds of convulsions. Zip-tied his wrists and ankles while he was still twitching. Duct tape over his mouth. Threw him in my trunk.

Then I drove him to my barn.

He woke up on the kill floor. Concrete. Drain. Plastic sheeting.

I let him see the tools first. Let his imagination do half the work.

Then I told him exactly why he was there.

I started with his hands. The ones that kept touching her after she safeworded.

Bolt cutters. Finger by finger. Left hand first.

He screamed so loud I thought the soundproofing might fail.

It didn't.

When all ten fingers were gone, I cauterized the stumps with a propane torch so he wouldn't bleed out too quickly.

Then I moved to what he'd used to violate her trust.

His cock.

I didn't cut it off—too quick, too merciful.

I'm hard again just remembering his screams.

The way he sobbed. The way he looked at me with those pleading eyes like I was the monster.

No.

He was the monster.

I am the scales of Justice

When he finally passed out from shock, I slit his throat and watched him bleed into the drain.

Dismembered the body. Burned the pieces in the wood furnace over three days.

Scattered the ashes in the national forest.

Derek doesn't exist anymore.

I return to the bed. Sit. Pick up the laptop.

The keystroke feed updates.

Question 5: What role does fear play in your arousal? Be specific.

I resume stroking. Slow pulls.

She types for three minutes straight.

Fear is central. Not terror—anticipatory fear. The fear of being pushed past her limits by someone who knows her capacity better than she does. Fear of being known. Fear of surrendering and loving it. Fear that wanting this makes her broken.

My cock throbs.

She's afraid of her own desires.

Afraid of the man who'll see through her defenses.

Afraid of how much she'll need what he gives her.

And the fear sharpens everything. Makes the surrender sweeter because she had to overcome something to get there.

I'm going to make her so fucking afraid.

Not of pain. Not of bondage. Of herself. Of how much she craves what I'm about to do to her. I'll push her right to the edge of her comfort zone and then one inch past it, watching her face in those mirrors while she realizes she doesn't want me to stop.

And when she's trembling, terrified of how good it feels, I'll make her say it out loud.

I'm afraid of how much I need this.

Question 6: Have you ever fantasized about someone manipulating circumstances to get close to you? Describe this fantasy.

I stop stroking.

Read her answer three times.

She fantasizes about orchestrated desperation. Someone creating the problem and offering himself as the solution. Watching her, studying her, learning everything. Manufacturing crisis so when he appears with rescue, she's grateful instead of suspicious.

By the time she realizes what he's done, she's already in too deep to leave.

And she doesn't want to leave.

The manipulation proves how much he wants her.

Being wanted so badly that someone would orchestrate her rescue makes her wet.

Wet.

I start stroking again. Faster now.

Question 7: What is your experience level with BDSM practices? What have you tried? What have you only imagined?

She understands the psychology but has never experienced it with someone she trusted.

She wants to.

I stroke faster.

Virgin territory.

Her body's been touched but her mind hasn't. Not really. Not by someone who knows what he's doing. Not by someone she can surrender to completely.

Every fantasy she's written, every scene she's researched obsessively, every psychological dynamic she understands in theory—I'm going to make real.

And she has no idea how intense it actually is.

How different fantasy feels when it's your wrists in real cuffs. Your throat under an actual hand. Your body bound to a table with your legs spread open.

She's going to discover the gap between imagination and reality.

I'm going to enjoy watching that discovery break her open.

Question 8: Describe your ideal dominant partner. What qualities matter most?

I read her answer and nearly come.

Someone who wants to own her mind, not just her body.

She just described me.

Perfectly.

And she has no idea she's about to meet the man she's been writing for years.

Question 9: What are you hoping to gain from this experience? Be honest.

Money first. Crisis management. Survival.

But underneath—she wants to know if it's real. If the dominance and surrender she fantasizes about actually exists or if it's just fiction. Wants to be completely controlled by someone competent. Wants to surrender everything by choice to someone worthy.

Wants one experience where she doesn't have to hide.

Wants to be seen.

My grip tightens.

She's going to get exactly what she's asking for.

And it's going to ruin her.

Question 10: What is your greatest fear about participating in this auction?

I slow my stroke. Read carefully.

She's afraid she can't handle it. Afraid she'll safeword immediately and prove she's a fraud.

Worse—afraid she'll love it so much that twenty-four hours won't be enough. Afraid it'll ruin her for normal relationships. Afraid it'll change her in ways she can't come back from.

Secret fear: what if the buyer is perfect, gives her everything, and then lets her go?

How does she survive that?

I stop stroking completely.

Stare at the screen.

She's afraid I'll be exactly what she needs.

And then I'll leave her.

My cock is painfully hard but I don't move. Don't breathe.

This is the vulnerability I've been looking for. The crack in her armor.

She doesn't fear inadequacy.

She fears perfection.

Fears finding exactly what she's been searching for and losing it after one taste.

I stroke myself slowly, staring at that last line.

How do I survive that?

You won't have to, my good little slut.

Because I'm not letting you go.

Not after one day. Not ever.

Christmas Eve is the beginning, not the end.

The form advances to Part II. Experience & Availability Menu.

I lean forward. This is what I've been waiting for. This is where she tells me exactly what I'm allowed to do to her.

Light bondage. Spanking. Blindfolds. Orgasm control. Temperature play.

She checks all five boxes. Basic. Expected. Nothing surprising yet.

Heavy bondage. She checks it. Moderate impact play. Checked. Complete sensory deprivation. Checked. Objectification. Checked.

Total Power Exchange—24 hours.

My breathing stops.

She checked it.

Twenty-four hours of absolute control. Every decision mine. Every moment choreographed to my specifications. She eats when I allow it. Sleeps when I permit it. Speaks when I command it.

She just gave me everything.

Psychological dominance. Mind games. Gaslighting desires. Using participant's own fantasies and writing against them. Checked.

My cock jumps.

She's giving me permission to weaponize her own words. Every story she's written. Every fantasy she's confessed in those questionnaire answers. I can use it all against her. Throw her darkest desires back in her face while she's restrained and helpless.

Forced confession. Verbalization of shameful desires under duress. Orgasm denial until honest.

Checked.

I'm going to make her say everything. Every filthy thought. Every degrading fantasy. Out loud. While looking at herself in those mirrors.

She wants to watch herself surrender. Wants to see her own face when she breaks.

Consensual non-consent—$50,000. Declined.

Public humiliation—$15,000. Declined.

Recording—$10,000. Declined.

Sharing—$25,000. Declined.

Extended captivity beyond contract duration—$20,000. Declined.

She left money on the table. Significant money. The CNC alone would've doubled her payout.

She declined because those scenarios require trust she doesn't have.

Yet.

Exhibitionism. Checked. Verbal degradation. Checked. Servitude. Checked. Sleep deprivation. Checked. Food control. Checked. Bathroom control. Checked.

And… unsurprisingly, forced orgasm until unconscious.

The form updates with a final summary page.

I read through her checked boxes one more time.

What she agreed to tells me who she is.

A woman who needs to surrender completely. Who craves being stripped down psychologically until there's nothing left to hide behind. Who wants to watch herself break.

What she declined tells me what she's afraid of.

She's afraid of losing autonomy permanently. Afraid of evidence. Afraid of this becoming something she can't walk away from.

But fear is just another tool.

I stroke faster. Tighter.

She just signed herself over to me.

Every humiliating confession I force from her lips —consensual.

Every orgasm I deny or force on her—agreed upon.

Every moment I make her watch herself in those mirrors while I degrade her—she checked the fucking box.

My breathing goes ragged.

My grip tightens. Pleasure builds at the base of my spine.

She declined CNC but checked psychological dominance.

Doesn't realize those overlap.

Doesn't understand that gaslighting her desires means

making her question what she actually wants. Making her beg for things she swore were limits. Making her so desperate, so broken down, that she'll agree to anything.

All consensual.

She signed the form.

I come hard, watching her cursor blink on the submission confirmation screen.

My release coats my hand, my stomach, my thighs.

I don't move. Don't clean up. Just sit there breathing while the pleasure rolls through me in waves.

She has no idea what she just agreed to.

No concept of how thoroughly I'm going to own her.

But she's about to learn.

CHAPTER 7
SCARLETTA

I stand in the lobby staring through the glass security door at the black limousine.

It's real.

This is actually happening.

The car is sleek, and black, and waiting. Engine running. Exhaust clouding in the freezing air.

I don't have to do this. I could turn around. Walk back up four flights. Lock myself in my blanket fort and pretend I never clicked that link.

Right. Back to your thrilling, adventurous existence filled with all those incredible opportunities and bright prospects stretching out before you.

My inner voice is particularly vicious tonight.

You've written about this exact scenario sixteen times. Every single one of them had a limousine. Remember "Claimed at Midnight" Chapter three? The car waiting in the snow while she decides whether to run?

She got in the car.

She surrendered.

It was the best decision she ever made.

Right. But that was fiction.

This is—

This is what you've been begging for in forty-seven stories. And now that it's here, you're going to chicken out?

My intellectual side kicks in, calm, and rational, and utterly unconvincing.

You're on step eleven. You gave them your entire sexual profile. Your address. Detailed sexual preferences. You got in the car three hours ago. You're already committed. Turning back now doesn't make you safe. It just makes you broke AND stupid.

The limousine idles.

Snow falls.

For the money, I tell myself.

Not for the sex.

For the money.

I push through the security door.

The cold hits me like a punch in the face. Wind. Snow. Idaho in December, brutal and unforgiving.

I take three steps toward the car and the driver's door opens. A man gets out. Forties, maybe. Clean-cut. Dark suit. He walks around the front of the limo with practiced efficiency and opens the rear passenger door.

He smiles at me. Warm. Professional. Like I'm a client, not a girl being delivered to—

Don't think about it.

He doesn't speak. Just holds the door and waits.

I gather what's left of my courage—which isn't much—and climb inside.

The door closes with a soft, final click.

I'm alone.

The interior is warm. Leather seats. Tinted windows. A screen built into the seat in front of me flickers to life as a video begins playing. Sleek production. Professional voiceover. A woman's voice, smooth and reassuring.

"Welcome to the Seventy-Fifth Annual Triple Xmas Auction. You are in professional hands."

The video shows the inside of the auction house. Not a dungeon. Not some dark basement.

It's gorgeous.

Floor-to-ceiling windows overlooking snow-covered mountains. Modern architecture. Clean lines. A massive stone fireplace in what looks like a lounge. Everything is cream, and gray, and polished wood. Expensive art on the walls. Leather furniture arranged in intimate groupings.

It looks like a luxury ski resort.

"Your safety, comfort, and consent are our top priorities. All participants have been thoroughly vetted. All benefactors have undergone extensive background checks and psychological evaluation."

The video cuts to sweeping aerial footage of the property —snow-draped peaks rising behind a sprawling estate, massive windows catching the afternoon light, smoke curling from stone chimneys. It's gorgeous. Intimidating. The kind of place people like me don't belong.

"Your experience will be tailored to the preferences you indicated in your intake form. Your buyer is under contract to adhere to your specific limits. Are you ready to have the experience of a lifetime? Are you ready to step into your future with enough money to never look back? If so, simply knock on the privacy divider when you are ready to proceed."

OK. Here goes nothing. I knock on the divider. Immediately, the car rolls smoothly forward. At the same time, the screen begins playing another video. Same calm voiceover.

"You are being transported to The Cheyenne Club Estate in Jackson, Wyoming. Your driver will take you to the FBO at Idaho Falls Regional Airport. Flight time is approximately fifteen minutes. Please relax and enjoy the journey."

It's a very specific message. Not generic. Not something they play for everyone. Unless they only choose girls from Idaho Falls, and somehow I find that hard to believe. Girls as dumb as me don't exist in concentration—you need to spread that net wide.

I would not call this realization comforting, but it does speak to the details. They made the message for *me*, and *only me*.

The car glides through dark streets as my thoughts spiral inward.

Four hours ago, I didn't even know I was in debt.

I mean, I did. Theoretically. In the abstract way you know the sun will eventually explode. Every single moment of my adult life has been spent drowning in various flavors of debt —student loans, credit cards, overdue rent, the slow suffocation of never having enough.

But it existed in the background, ambient dread I'd learned to tune out like tinnitus.

Now, I'm on my way to Jackson—a place normal people like me *do not go*, where billionaires park their private jets and buy second homes they visit twice a year—so I can sell my body, my boundaries, and my sexual fantasies to the highest bidder for forty-four thousand dollars.

Forty-four thousand dollars that will evaporate the moment it touches my bank account, swallowed whole by the endless maw of debt I've accumulated through a combination of bad decisions, worse luck, and the fundamental inability to function like a responsible adult.

All right. Enough already, my snarky inner monologue snaps, sharp and defensive. *You've established the premise.*

You're poor, you're desperate, you're fucked. You're dumb enough to get in a stranger's car, naive enough to sign a contract probably overflowing with fine print, and broken enough to think selling yourself is a viable solution to your problems. You're gonna be killed, probably. Dismembered. Disappeared. You're long past cautionary tale and well into tragic ending territory.

Try and enjoy it, for the sake of fuck.

The chuckle burbles up out of me unbidden.

Sake of fuck. Only my writer brain—

The car stops.

I blink. Look out the window. We're not at an airport.

We're on the edge of a dark runway. A single building off to the side, all glass and steel, lit from within. Beyond it—

Oh God.

A helicopter.

Rotors spinning. That low, thudding sound that vibrates through your chest. Red and white lights blinking against the night sky.

The driver opens my door.

Cold air rushes in. Snow. Wind. The deafening roar of instant karma.

I don't move.

Get out of the car, Scarletta.

I can't.

You've come this far. Get. Out.

My legs work without permission. I climb out. Stand on the tarmac. The wind tears at my clothes, whipping hair across my face.

A man appears beside me. Dark coat. Headset. He's yelling something but I can't hear him over the rotors. His mouth moves. Words I can't process.

He gestures toward the helicopter.

I shake my head.

He grabs my elbow—not rough, just firm—and tugs me forward.

My feet move. One step. Two. The noise gets louder. The wind stronger. I'm walking toward a helicopter. I'm getting on a helicopter.

You're going to die. This is it. They're going to throw you out over the mountains and no one will ever find your body.

The rational part of my brain is screaming that this is insane. That normal sex auctions don't involve helicopters. That I should run. That I should—

The man opens the door and practically lifts me inside.

The interior is—

I don't know what I expected. Cramped seats and exposed machinery, maybe. Military transport. Utilitarian.

This is not that.

The space is tall enough to stand in. Cream leather seats arranged in pairs facing each other. A single chair positioned near the front. Large rectangular windows lining both sides. A closed door at the back that has to be a bathroom.

Everything is cream, and tan, and polished wood. Clean lines. Expensive materials. More space than seems necessary for one person.

Of course it is. Because billionaires don't fly coach.

The pilot turns in his seat. Looks at me. Points at one of the cream leather seats and then at the seatbelt.

"Buckle in," he yells over the noise.

I nod. Autopilot. I walk to the nearest seat—my legs shaking, my hands numb—and collapse into leather so soft it feels obscene.

The door closes.

The noise drops to a manageable roar.

I fumble with the seatbelt. Four-point harness. My fingers are clumsy. Frozen. Useless.

Click. Click. Click. Click.

The lights dim, the roar deepens, then a piercing whine as the helicopter lifts.

My stomach drops. The ground falls away beneath us and

suddenly we're rising, tilting forward, and Idaho Falls spreads out below like a circuit board. Lights. Streets. Buildings getting smaller and smaller.

I press my face against the window.

The city shrinks. The darkness expands.

We're flying over nothing now. Mountains. Snow. Endless black punctuated by the occasional cluster of lights that might be a town, or might be a ranch, or might be nothing at all.

You're in a helicopter, my brain informs me, as if I've just woken from a dream and need the commentary. *Flying to Wyoming. To sell your body to a stranger who will pay forty-four thousand dollars for twenty-four hours with you.*

The helicopter banks left and my stomach lurches. I've got a death-grip on the armrests.

Below us, the world is dark, and cold, and completely indifferent to whether I live or die.

Just a few minutes later, a new cluster of lights appear below. Bigger than the scattered ranches we've been passing. More organized. Streets laid out in grids.

Jackson.

I press my face harder against the window, breath fogging the glass.

But the helicopter doesn't descend toward the town where the sun is just about to rise on the eastern edge. It banks left, following a valley that cuts deeper into the mountains. Away from civilization. Away from witnesses.

Of course. Because whatever happens next needs to happen where no one can hear you scream.

The lights below change. Not a town anymore. Something else.

A building. No, *buildings.* Multiple structures connected by covered walkways, all lit from within. Modern architecture mixed with rustic timber. Floor-to-ceiling windows glowing warm against the snow. A circular driveway.

The Cheyenne Club.

It looks like a luxury ski resort. Like somewhere you'd have a romantic weekend with someone you're trying to impress. Not like—whatever this is.

The helicopter descends. My stomach rises into my throat. We're dropping fast, the buildings getting bigger, closer, and then we're hovering over a helipad marked with a giant illuminated X.

The skids touch down. Gentle. Barely a bump.

The rotors begin to slow.

I can't move.

Unbuckle your seatbelt, Scarletta. This is what you signed up for. This is—

The door opens.

Cold air rushes in. A man in a dark suit stands in the opening, one hand extended toward me. White gloves. Perfect posture. He's probably fifty, graying at the temples, with the kind of face that doesn't smile but doesn't need to.

"Miss," he says. His voice is loud, but smooth. Professional. Like this is completely normal. "Welcome to the Cheyenne Club. I'm Mr. Fitzwilliam. If you'll allow me."

I stare at his hand.

He doesn't lower it.

My fingers fumble with the seatbelt. Four-point harness. Release. Click. Click. Click. Click.

I take his hand.

His grip is firm as he helps me stand, guides me toward the door. The wind hits immediately—freezing, sharp, stealing my breath. My shoes touch the helipad. Solid ground. I'm shaking.

Mr. Fitzwilliam's hand moves to my elbow. Not aggressive. Just—controlled. The way you'd guide a child who might bolt.

"This way, please."

He walks. I follow because his hand on my elbow gives me no other choice.

The helipad connects to a covered walkway. Glass walls on both sides. Heated. The transition from freezing wind to warm air makes my skin prickle.

Through the glass I can see the main building. Massive timber beams. Stone. Windows that show glimpses of leather furniture and fireplaces and—

"The preparation suite is just ahead," Mr. Fitzwilliam says.

Preparation suite?

We turn left. Another hallway. Smaller. More private. He opens a door and guides me inside.

The room is—

Not what I expected.

Soft lighting. Cream walls. A massage table in the center draped in white linens. Cabinets along one wall. A vanity with a lit mirror. Silk robe hanging on a hook. Everything smells like eucalyptus and something else I can't identify. Something expensive.

Three men appear from a door I didn't notice. Young. Maybe late twenties. They're all wearing white linen—pants, button-down shirts that look soft and expensive. No shoes. They move like dancers. Graceful and synchronized.

They smile at me.

Not predatory smiles. Gentle ones. Like I'm a nervous animal they need to calm.

Mr. Fitzwilliam's hand leaves my elbow. "Enjoy the next four hours, Miss. You're in excellent hands."

Then he's gone. The door closes with a soft click.

I'm alone with three strange men in a room.

Four hours? What the fuck happens in here for four hours?

"So," I say, my voice too loud in the quiet space. "This is where you harvest my organs, right? I mean, statistically, I'm worth more in parts than—"

The tallest one—dark hair, warm brown eyes—puts a finger to his lips. Gentle. Shushing me like you'd quiet a crying baby. He's not smiling anymore but his eyes are kind.

They move closer as a trio. Surrounding me in a triangle formation.

"Wait, I—"

Hands touch my shoulders. Not grabbing. Just—there. The tall one in front of me. His fingers find the zipper of my hoodie. He pulls the zipper down.

"I can—I can do that myself—"

Another soft shush. This one from behind me. A different voice. Lower.

The hoodie slides off my shoulders. Someone takes it from me. Folds it. Sets it on a chair like it's not a ratty piece of garbage I've been living in for days.

The one with blonde hair kneels. His hands find the waistband of my leggings.

Oh god.

"Wait—"

He looks up at me. Blue eyes. Still gentle. Still kind.

He doesn't wait.

He pulls my leggings down. I'm not wearing underwear because I haven't done laundry in three weeks and I ran out and—

Jesus Christ, Scarletta. You're standing in front of three strange men and you're not wearing underwear.

The leggings pool at my ankles. Someone lifts my left foot. Then my right. The fabric disappears.

I'm naked except for my bra. Sports bra. Gray. The elastic is shot. One of the straps is held together with a safety pin.

The tall one reaches around my back. Finds the clasp.

"I really don't think—"

Shush.

The bra falls away.

I'm completely naked.

I should cover myself. Cross my arms over my breasts. Put my hands between my legs. But I'm frozen. Paralyzed. Three men are looking at me and I can't move and I can't breathe and—

Hands touch my elbow. Guiding me. Not forcing. Just—moving me.

There's a tub. I didn't see it before. How did I not see it before?

It's massive. Freestanding. Oval. Carved from a single piece of white marble that looks like it was stolen from a Roman bathhouse. Steam rises from the surface.

They guide me to the edge. I step up onto a small platform. The tall one takes my hand. Steadying me.

I lower one foot into the water.

It's perfect.

Not too hot. Exactly right. The kind of temperature that makes your muscles unclench before you realize they were clenched.

I sink lower. The water rises around my calves, my thighs, my hips. Someone's hand stays on my elbow until I'm sitting, submerged to my shoulders.

The heat hits me everywhere at once. My skin flushes. My heartbeat slows.

When was the last time you took a bath? When was the last time you —

Hands touch my hair. Gentle fingers working through the tangled mess. I haven't brushed it in—

Don't think about that. Don't think about how disgusting you are.

Water pours over my head. Warm. Someone's using a pitcher or a cup, rinsing my hair, smoothing it back from my face.

Something floral-scented. Shampoo. Expensive shampoo that doesn't smell like synthetic fruit. Hands massage my scalp. Working the lather through. Fingers finding every knot, every tangle, patiently working them loose.

I close my eyes.

This is insane. You're insane. Three strange men are washing your hair and you're just—sitting here. Letting them.

More water. Rinsing. The shampoo swirls away.

Then conditioner. Thicker. Silkier. They work it through the ends of my hair, patient with every snarl.

A hand appears in front of my face holding a white washcloth. Soft. Probably Egyptian cotton or some shit I can't afford.

The blonde one kneels beside the tub. He dips the cloth in the water, adds something from a bottle—body wash that smells like jasmine and something darker, richer—and begins washing my arm.

Long strokes. Methodical. He lifts my wrist, turns my hand over, washes my palm, between my fingers.

The one behind me washes my back. Shoulders. Spine. The small of my back.

The third one washes my other arm.

They don't speak. Don't explain. Just clean me.

The washcloth moves to my collarbone. My throat. Down between my breasts.

I should say something. Stop this. But my mouth won't work.

The cloth slides lower. Over my ribs. My stomach. The soft flesh I hide under oversized hoodies.

Lower.

CHAPTER 8
CALEB

The Master Suite lives up to its name.

Sixteen monitors mounted on the mahogany-paneled wall, each showing a different woman in various stages of preparation. Some crying. Some defiant. One laughing nervously with her attendants like this is a spa day and not exactly what it is.

I'm not interested in fifteen of them.

The other panel of monitors—all six that I've configured myself—show different angles of Scarletta's preparation suite. Camera one: wide shot of the entire bathroom. Camera two: close-up of the tub. Camera three: overhead view. Camera four: profile angle. Cameras five and six I can control manually, zooming and panning as needed.

Right now, I need camera two.

The washcloth has traveled south. Between her legs. The blonde one—I should've gotten his name, tipped him extra— moves with professional efficiency. Not groping. Not violating boundaries. Just washing.

Thoroughly.

Scarletta's eyes go wide. Her mouth opens slightly. I watch her chest rise and fall faster.

She doesn't stop them.

Doesn't close her legs, doesn't push his hand away, doesn't say a word.

The cloth slides over her pussy. Once. Twice. A third time that lingers.

Her thighs part slightly.

There it is.

I zoom camera two until I can see the flush spreading across her chest, the way her nipples have gone hard, the slight tremor in her breathing.

She's written this scene seventeen times across her portfolio. Different setups—kidnapped and bathed by her captor's servants, prepared for a wedding night by handmaidens, cleansed before a ritual. The details change but the core fantasy stays consistent: being touched by strangers while powerless to stop it, shame and arousal tangled so tightly she can't separate them.

In "The Arrangement," her protagonist Isla is bathed by three male servants before being presented to a warlord.

They wash between my legs with detached aloofness, but there's nothing aloof or detached about my body's response. I'm wet and it's not from the bathwater. One of them notices. I see it in his eyes —a flicker of knowledge that makes my face burn. He doesn't comment. Just continues washing me like I'm an object being prepared for use. Which I am. God help me, which I am. And my body doesn't care about the shame. My body wants.

Scarletta moans softly on screen.

Not loud. Not performative. A small sound that escapes before she can stop it.

The attendants lift her from the tub. Water drips down her body. She's shivering despite the room's warmth. They wrap her in heated towels, patting her dry with the same methodical care they used washing her.

Then they guide her to the massage table as I adjust the cameras to the new location.

It's positioned perfectly in frame. I made sure of it when I arranged the camera installations, when I specified exactly which preparation room she'd be assigned to and what would be done to her there.

She lies face-up on the table. White marble surface. Heated from below. The towels disappear.

She's naked again. Completely exposed under the soft lighting.

One attendant produces a bottle of oil. Pours it into his palms, rubs them together. The scent would be jasmine and sandalwood—I specified the blend myself, matched it to what she uses in her stories.

His hands start at her shoulders. Kneading. Working the tension from muscles that have been clenched for years.

She makes another small sound. Relief this time. Her eyes close.

The other two join him. Six hands moving over her body. Professional massage techniques designed to awaken every nerve ending, to make skin hypersensitive, to prepare a body for touch that comes later.

They're fluffers. That's the industry term. Getting her aroused, primed, ready for whoever wins her.

Except there's no "whoever." There's only me.

I've already won. She just doesn't know it yet.

The hands move lower. Over her ribs. Her stomach. The soft flesh she hides under oversized hoodies. One attendant works her arms, pulling each one overhead, stretching her out. Another focuses on her legs, starting at her ankles and moving up her calves.

The third one—the quiet one with dark hair—pours more oil directly onto her chest.

It pools between her breasts. He smooths it outward with both palms. Covering her completely. His hands shape themselves to her curves, professional but thorough. Cupping the weight of each breast, thumbs circling but not quite touching her nipples.

Scarletta's breathing changes. Faster. Shallower.

She keeps her eyes closed. Probably telling herself this is just a massage. Just preparation. Nothing sexual about oil-slicked hands on her naked tits.

Liar.

Her nipples are hard. I can see them clearly on camera two. Flushed dark pink, peaked, begging for attention those hands won't give.

Not their job. Their job is to make her desperate for it.

The attendant working her legs has reached her inner thighs. His hands slide higher with each stroke. Oil makes his palms glide smoothly over her skin. He pushes her legs wider apart—just slightly, just enough—and his thumbs press into the crease where thigh meets hip.

So close to her pussy but not touching.

She shifts on the table. Small movement. Unconscious. Her hips tilt upward maybe an inch.

Seeking.

Camera four gives me the perfect angle. I can see between her legs. Can see she's wet. Not from the bath. From this. From the hands of strangers all over her body, positioning her, spreading her, taking away her choices.

Just like she's written it.

In "Captive," the protagonist Elena is prepared for her first night with her kidnapper. Three servants bathe and oil her. Scarletta spent four thousand words on that scene. Describing every touch, every moment of mounting arousal, the shame of being turned on by violation.

I shouldn't be wet. I shouldn't want this. But their hands know exactly where to touch, where to avoid, how to make my body betray me. One of them works his fingers closer to where I'm aching and I hate myself for hoping he'll slip, hoping he'll give me what I need, hoping—

God, what's wrong with me?

On screen, Scarletta bites her lip.

The dark-haired attendant has moved from her breasts to her stomach. Long strokes down her centerline. Each one ending just above her blonde mound. His fingers splay wide, covering her from hip to hip, pressing in as he draws his hands downward.

Again.

Again.

Never quite touching her pussy but promising he might.

Her thighs fall open wider.

She's stopped pretending this is just a massage.

The attendant working her legs slides both hands up the inside of her thighs simultaneously. Firm pressure. Spreading her further. His thumbs meet at her apex—so close I can see her pussy clench in anticipation—and then trace outward along her hip bones.

Scarletta whimpers.

An actual whimper. Needy and desperate and so fucking beautiful I have to adjust my cock through my slacks.

The third attendant—the blond—moves to her head. Tilts it back slightly. Begins massaging her temples, her jaw, her throat. Long strokes down the column of her neck. His fingers trail over her collarbones, down between her breasts, connecting to where the dark-haired one is working her stomach.

These men are experts at what they do. The whole thing comes off as choreography. They probably prepare a dozen women a season this way, getting them trembling, and wet, and ready to be fucked.

But none of those women wrote the instruction manual.

Scarletta did. Every scene she's ever written is a blueprint of her psychology, a map of her nervous system, a detailed guide on how to unmake her.

And I've studied that guide for six months.

The dark-haired attendant's hands dip lower. Not between her legs—not yet—but to the crease where thigh meets torso. Pressing. Massaging. His thumbs so close to her pussy she *has* to feel his body heat.

Her hips lift again. More obvious this time. Seeking contact he won't give.

I was wrong. They're not just fluffers.

They're talented sadists.

The one working her legs spreads them wider. Bends her knees. Plants her feet flat on the table with her thighs butterflied open.

Camera two shows me everything. Her pussy fully exposed. Glistening. Swollen. Pink, and pretty, and desperate for attention.

One of them pours more oil. It drips onto her inner thigh. Warm. Trickling downward toward—

She gasps.

The attendant catches the oil with his palm before it reaches her pussy. Smooths it along her thigh instead. Slides both hands up and down her legs, getting closer with each pass but never arriving.

Scarletta's fingers grip the edges of the massage table. Her knuckles go white.

She wants them to touch her. Wants it badly enough that shame doesn't matter anymore, that the audience of three strangers doesn't matter, that whatever dignity she arrived with has dissolved in jasmine-scented oil and mounting desperation.

The blond attendant moves to her breasts again. This time his palms slide directly over her nipples. Circling. Applying pressure. Not quite pinching but close enough to make her arch into his hands.

Her mouth falls open. No sound comes out but I can see her throat working, can see her trying not to moan.

The dark-haired one traces patterns on her stomach.

Figure-eights. Spirals. Each one dipping lower until his fingertips brush the top of her mound.

Still not touching her clit. Still making her wait.

She's written this exact torture in nine different stories. The anticipation that's worse than the act. The build-up that makes eventual release feel like transcendence.

I unbuckle my belt. Unzip my slacks. My cock is hard enough to hurt, straining against my boxer briefs.

I don't want to jerk off. Not when I'm just a few hours away from having her myself. Not when I've waited six months for the real thing.

But I pull my cock out anyway.

Because watching her surrender is a major part of the game for me.

The attendant working her legs slides his hands up her inner thighs one more time. This time his thumbs bracket her pussy. Pressing into the soft flesh on either side. So close she has to feel his breath on her wet skin.

He holds that position. Just—holds it.

Scarletta's entire body goes tense. Waiting. Trembling.

Then he pulls away.

She makes a sound. Frustrated. Almost angry.

I wrap my hand around my cock and stroke slowly.

All three attendants step back from the table in synchronized movement. Leaving her spread open, and untouched, and visibly aching.

Beautiful.

The blond one produces a white silk robe. They help her sit up—she's unsteady, disoriented—and guide her arms into the sleeves.

She doesn't want the robe. She wants their hands back on her body. Wants someone to finish what they started.

I can see it in every line of her posture. The way she stands too still, thighs pressed together, trying to create friction. The flush that hasn't faded from her chest. The rapid breathing that has nothing to do with exertion.

They tie the robe closed. Cover her completely.

Then the dark-haired attendant's hand slips beneath the silk.

I zoom camera two.

His hand moves between her legs. I can't see his fingers but I can see the movement of his wrist. Slow circles. Deliberate pressure.

Scarletta's head falls back. Her mouth opens. Her hips roll forward into his touch as the other two hold her up.

Finally. Finally they're giving her what she needs.

His other hand covers her breast through the silk. Squeezing. Thumb circling her nipple.

She's going to come. Right there in the middle of the room with three strangers pleasuring her like it's their job.

Because it *is* their job.

My hand moves faster on my cock. I'm close. Too close. But I can't stop watching.

The attendant's wrist moves faster. More pressure. Scarletta's thighs start to shake. Her hands grip his shoulders for balance. Small sounds escape her throat—need, and shame, and surrender all tangled together.

She's almost there. I can see it. The tension building in her body, the way her breathing goes ragged, the moment before—

She bites her lip. Hard. Her whole body goes rigid.

And she holds it there. Trembling on the edge. Refusing to fall.

The attendant keeps touching her but she's fighting it. Fighting her own body's need to release.

Denying herself.

Jesus Christ.

I come so hard my vision goes white. Hot semen spilling

over my fist, my cock pulsing, her name almost escaping my throat before I catch it.

"Good girl," I breathe instead. "Such a good girl."

Saving herself for me even when she doesn't know it yet.

My good little slut.

She's going to be the death of me.

Or maybe I'll be the death of her.

CHAPTER 9
SCARLETTA

I'm standing in the middle of the preparation suite, thighs pressed together so hard they're shaking, silk robe sticking to my oiled skin, trying—*trying*—not to come just from the memory of their hands on me.

This is who I am. This is what I've become.

A girl who almost came in the middle of a room, being held up by strangers, while one of them touched her like she was livestock being checked for market.

Because that's exactly what you are. Livestock. Product. A thing being sold.

My clit is throbbing. Actually throbbing. I can feel my pulse between my legs, this awful desperate ache that won't go away no matter how still I stand.

I should be horrified. I should be disgusted with myself.

But all I can think about is how close I was. How badly I wanted to let go. How much I *still* want to let go.

Pathetic. You're pathetic.

The three attendants circle me. Like I'm prey. Like they know exactly what I'm feeling and they're enjoying it.

The blonde one leans in first. His lips brush my cheek—

gentle, almost affectionate—and he whispers, "It's okay if you come next time. We're paid to fluff you up."

Fluff you up.

Like I'm a pillow. Like I'm a product that needs to be presented at peak condition.

My face burns. Shame floods through me so hot I think I might actually combust right here on this eucalyptus-scented floor.

The second attendant—dark hair, the one who had his fingers on my clit, kisses my other cheek. "The buyers like the girls ready and wanting."

Ready and wanting.

I am. God help me, I am.

The third one, the quiet one who worked my legs, kisses my forehead this time. His voice is softer. Almost kind. "See you next month."

He moves away before I can process what he said.

Next month?

Next month?

What does that—

"Thank you, gentlemen. That will be all." Mr. Fitzwilliam appears in the doorway, clapping his hands twice. Sharp. Efficient.

They file out past him without looking back.

Mr. Fitzwilliam turns to me, adjusting his perfect cuffs. "Miss Desmond. It's nearly your turn at the auction. If you'll follow me, please."

I stare at him. My brain isn't working. Nothing is computing.

"I—four hours? It's been four hours already?" How the hell could four hours have passed? Did I fall asleep in the tub and not realize it?

"Slightly over four hours, yes." Fitzwilliams says, checking his watch. "The bidding is running behind due to an unforeseen circumstance, but we should move you into position regardless."

Unforeseen circumstance.

I want to ask what that means. I want to know what kind of unforeseen circumstance delays a sex auction. I want to know if someone got hurt, or if someone backed out, or if—

But I don't ask.

Because I'm afraid of the answer.

Because whatever the answer is, I'm still going to walk through that door. I'm still going to let them auction me off like a piece of meat. I'm still going to let some stranger buy the right to touch me however he wants for forty-four thousand dollars.

See you next month.

Mr. Fitzwilliam extends his hand toward the doorway. "Miss Desmond?"

I follow him.

Because that's what I do. Apparently.

The hallway beyond is all glass and polished wood. I can hear music now. Voices. The low murmur of wealthy people doing wealthy things.

My pussy is still wet. Still aching.

And I'm walking toward the room where they're going to sell me.

Mr. Fitzwilliam opens a door like he's unveiling something precious. Like I should be grateful for what's on the other side.

I step through.

Velvet chairs line the walls. Deep burgundy. The kind you see in old theaters where people used to watch plays about tragic women who died beautifully.

Two girls already occupy the space.

Girls. Not women. Girls who look like they'd need fake IDs to get into bars. One perched on the edge of her chair, fingers knotted together so tight her knuckles are white. The other sprawled back with her legs crossed, examining her cuticles like she's waiting for a bus.

Three white silk robes. Three participants.

Three pieces of livestock.

My hand moves automatically toward my pocket. Toward the familiar weight of my phone—it's not there.

I left it in the preparation suite. Or they took it. I can't remember which. The last four hours are already blurring together like watercolor left out in the rain.

I raise one finger toward Mr. Fitzwilliam. "My phone? I think I left it—"

His head moves once. A single shake. No.

He exits. The door clicks.

The girl examining her nails speaks without looking up. "They keep the phones. Buyers get them temporarily. It's in the contract. You'll get it back after."

She shifts her attention to the nervous girl. Her voice stays flat. Bored. "What did you check this time? I had to pick the scat." She crinkles her nose. "But it's like fifteen grand, so..."

Her words trail off.

This time.

Not *this one desperate choice.* Not *this mistake I'll never repeat.*

This *time.* Like there's been other times. Like there will be more times.

The nervous girl's voice barely carries across the room. "I'm down to CNC. But it's fifty thousand, right? Totally worth it, right?"

Consensual non-consent. The highest-value option on the menu. The one I couldn't even consider without my stomach turning inside out.

The bored girl nods like they're discussing whether to get pizza or Chinese food. "Yeah. Mine was..." She blows out a breath. "Like... wow."

"You liked it?" the scared girl asks.

Confident girl mouths the words, "Loved it," without making any sound.

The scared girl looks at me. Tears forming in her eyes. "Did you ever do it?"

I shake my head no, unable to speak.

She goes back to looking at her feet.

A woman appears in the doorway. Severe features. Hair pulled back so tight it must hurt. Disappointment carved into every line of her face like she's been let down by absolutely everyone she's ever met.

She holds a clipboard. "Arabella Wilde."

Arabella Wilde.

The name sounds borrowed from a fantasy novel. Not real. Not something anyone would put on a birth certificate.

The trembling girl stands. Her legs look like they might give out. Fear rolls off her in waves I can actually feel from here.

She follows the severe woman through the opposite door anyway.

The door closes.

Two of us remain.

Silence settles over the room like dust. Heavy. Suffocating.

The confident girl's eyes lock with mine from across the room. Direct eye contact.

Questions pile up in my throat. But I can't ask any of them. Because I'm terrified of the answers.

Her mouth curves upward. Not quite a smile. "So what'd you check? Got anything fun going this time? How much you gonna make?"

I swallow. "Um. Not really. Forced confession. Total power exchange."

Her laughter fills the small room. Sharp. Mocking. "TPE? You checked *TPE?* That's like a thousand bucks." She shakes her head. "Not worth it, my friend No. Absolutely not.

Fucking newbies. Showing up with their little sex fantasies like this is a boyfriend experience."

My face burns.

Little sex fantasies.

It hurts because… it's true.

Mean lady is back.

"Already?" I ask. Surprised the last girl's auction went so quick.

Confident girl is already standing, like she can't wait to play with scat. She looks at me as she passes. "Oh, rape fantasies are pre-arranged. The auction was fake."

Then she walks out.

I'm alone.

The confident girl is gone. The terrified girl is gone. Just me and my burning face and the way my heart won't stop hammering against my ribs.

The auction was fake.

What does that mean? What does—

I can't finish the thought. My brain's moving too fast, skipping like a scratched CD over the same three seconds of panic.

Forty-four thousand dollars. Total Power Exchange. Forced confession. Using my own writing against me.

Little sex fantasies.

She laughed at me. She actually laughed.

"I'm so stupid," I whisper to the empty room. "I'm so fucking stupid."

My voice sounds small. Pathetic.

I should've checked CNC. I should've checked everything. Fifty thousand dollars would've—

Would've what? Made you less of a whore?

I press my palms against my eyes. Hard enough to see stars.

"This is fine. This is totally fine. You made your choice. You signed the forms. You let three strangers touch you and you almost came in front of them like some kind of—"

Something catches my eye.

Small. Dark. Mounted in the corner where the wall meets the ceiling.

A camera.

My stomach drops.

There's another one. Above the door. And another behind the velvet chair. And—

Oh god.

They're everywhere.

Four. Five. Six cameras that I can see, which means there are probably more I can't.

People are watching me right now.

Right now, while I'm standing here in this silk robe talking to myself like a crazy person, someone is watching.

Multiple someones.

My breath comes faster. Shallow. My vision tunnels at the edges.

Were they watching during the preparation? Were they watching while those men bathed me? While they touched me? While I almost—

Of course they were watching. That's the whole point. You're the product. They need to see the product.

Heat floods through me. Shame so thick I can taste it.

But underneath the shame, something else.

Something worse.

I'm wet.

I'm wet, and my nipples are hard, and there's this awful pulse between my legs that won't stop.

You're turned on.

No. No, I'm not. I'm terrified. I'm humiliated. I'm—

The questionnaire.

There was a question about this. About being watched without consent. About the fantasy of surveillance.

Did I check that box?

I can't remember. I can't fucking remember.

My hands are shaking. I clench them into fists, trying to ground myself, but it doesn't help.

The door opens.

Severe woman. Clipboard. That same expression like I've personally disappointed her just by existing.

"Scarletta Mae Desmond."

She uses my real name.

My actual, legal, *real* name.

Not a fantasy novel name. Not code name whatever. Just me. My legs don't feel attached to my body.

She doesn't wait. She turns and walks.

I follow.

The hallway is longer than I expected. White walls. Soft lighting. Classical music playing from speakers I can't see.

It should be comforting. It's not.

We stop at a heavy wooden door.

She turns to face me. I expect to see something—anticipation, maybe contempt, the faintest flicker of humanity—but her voice arrives perfectly flat and mechanical. Rehearsed to the point of automation.

"Enter the stage. Walk directly to the raised platform. Stand precisely in the center on the marked position. Remove your robe completely—no hesitation, no false modesty. Once naked, turn slowly in a full circle so the prospective buyers can assess you from every angle. Pause at each quarter turn for approximately three seconds."

She pauses, studying my face with that same clinical detachment. Waiting.

"Do you understand these instructions?"

I open my mouth. Nothing comes out.

"Do you understand?" she repeats.

"Yes."

"Good."

She opens the door.

Music swells. String instruments and something else I can't identify.

I step through.

The room beyond is massive. Theater-style seating rises in curved rows, all facing a raised platform with a single spotlight aimed at its center.

Masked men fill the seats. Dozens of them. Maybe fifty. Maybe more. They're wearing masquerade-type masks. The black kind that only cover your eyes and do nothing to actually hide who you are. They're all wearing tuxedos. All watching the door I just walked through.

All watching *me*.

My feet move. I don't tell them to. They just move.

One step. Another. The platform is three steps up.

I climb them.

The spotlight finds me immediately. Hot and blinding.

I can't see the men anymore. Just shapes in the darkness beyond the light.

There's a marker on the floor. A small circle of tape.

I stand on it.

My hands find the silk tie at my waist. I pull.

The robe falls.

I'm naked.

Completely, totally naked in front of fifty strangers who paid to be here.

Who paid to see me.

I turn. Pause. Turn. Pause. Turn. Pause. Last turn. Stand.

A voice comes through speakers. Male. Smooth. Professional.

"Lot Number Twelve. Scarletta Mae Desmond. Age twenty-two. Five feet six inches. One hundred eighteen pounds. Measurements thirty-four, twenty-four, thirty-five. Bachelor's degree in English Literature from Boise State University. Currently unemployed."

Currently unemployed.

Like that's a selling point.

"Miss Desmond's hobbies include writing original erotica on the popular forum DarkDesires under the pseudonym ScarletSins. Her portfolio contains forty-seven completed works exploring themes of captivity, psychological dominance, and forced confession."

No.

No.

"Notable titles include 'Prey,' 'The Arrangement,' 'Captive,' and 'See Me, Spank Me, Cure Me.' Her work demonstrates a sophisticated understanding of power dynamics and submission psychology."

This isn't happening.

This can't be—

"From her story 'Owned by the Slave Trader,' Chapter Seventeen: 'His hand wrapped around my throat and I stopped breathing. Not because he was choking me. Because for the first time in my life, someone saw the dark parts and didn't look away.'"

He's quoting me. Actual lines from my work. On, and on, and on… He's reading my actual words to a room full of men who—

"Miss Desmond's intake questionnaire reveals fantasies including twenty-four-hour Total Power Exchange, forced confession, verbal degradation, and permission for her buyer to weaponize her own writing against her."

My face is burning. My whole body is burning.

"Buyers should refer to page twelve of your programs for complete details regarding Miss Desmond's selected activities and boundaries."

There's rustling. The sound of pages turning.

They're reading about me. About what I want. About what I'm willing to let them do.

The announcer's voice softens. Almost intimate.

"Gentlemen. What you're bidding on tonight isn't just a body. It's a mind. A rare and remarkable mind that understands submission not as weakness but as the ultimate act of trust. Miss Desmond doesn't just write about surrender. She craves it. Studies it. Dreams about it."

I'm going to be sick.

"The bidding begins at one-hundred thousand dollars."

CHAPTER 10
CALEB

I watch from my cabin's control room, leather chair angled toward the wall of monitors, Macallan Twenty-Five in a crystal tumbler resting against my thigh.

My helicopter dropped me here thirty minutes ago, then returned to the club for Scarletta. She'll be delivered to me like a package. Gift-wrapped in humiliation and fear.

Exactly as planned.

Six screens show Scarletta's auction from different angles. Close-ups of her face. Wide shots of the theater. Overhead view of the platform where she stands naked under that spotlight, trying not to shake.

She's shaking anyway.

The other nine screens cycle through the other auction rooms. Sixteen girls total tonight. All of them already owned. All of them thinking this is real.

It's theater. Expensive, elaborate, legally binding theater that was specifically designed for them.

Every girl signed contracts agreeing to specific acts. Every girl walked onto a stage believing strangers would bid on her body. Every girl will leave with a man who's been watching her for months.

The auctions are pretense. The paperwork is deliciously confusing.

The result, always the same.

They understand.

Yet, they don't.

They understand what they agreed to, but it's set up.

A tiny lie of omission. Still legal, *if* things like this were legal, that is.

They're not. Not in the world Scarletta lives in, at least.

But in my world… *in my world*, they absolutely are.

I take another sip of whiskey. Smooth. Expensive. Celebratory.

On screen, the announcer begins reading Scarletta's details. Height, weight, measurements. Her *unemployment status* delivered with just enough emphasis to remind everyone watching that she's desperate.

I wrote that line myself.

Gave the announcer a script. Told him which stories to quote, which passages would cut deepest. Made sure he understood the goal wasn't just to sell her body—it was to strip away every defense she'd built between herself and her shame.

She checked the box for verbal degradation. For psychological dominance. For permission to weaponize her writing against her.

I'm simply honoring her contract.

The announcer's voice drops into a different register—intimate, almost reverent—as he begins to recite passages I selected myself. Lines from "Owned by the Slave Trader," that story she posted at three in the morning nine weeks ago. The one where her protagonist begs to be seen completely, darkness and all.

"'I want hands that know how to hurt me,'" he reads, letting each word land with deliberate weight. "'Not because I deserve pain, but because pain is the only thing that feels honest anymore.'"

Scarletta's breathing changes. I can see it on the monitor, the way her chest rises faster, shallower.

He continues. "'Choke me until the world goes quiet. Hold me down until I stop pretending I don't want this. Make me admit what I am.'"

Her own words. Her own need, stripped bare and broadcast to strangers.

The announcer pauses for effect—I told him to do that, let the silence build—before delivering the final passage. "'I don't want someone who loves me despite the darkness. I want someone who loves me because of it.'"

On the close-up monitor, Scarletta's face goes white. Then red.

She didn't expect this. Thought "weaponize your writing" meant teasing her about a sexy story during foreplay.

No.

It means this.

Fifty men—actors, props, fluffers paid to fill seats and look interested—listening to her most private fantasies read aloud like livestock specifications.

She's learning the difference between fantasy and reality.

She's learning what she agreed to.

The announcer continues. Scarletta stands frozen in the spotlight, naked and exposed, while her psychological profile gets dissected for an audience that doesn't exist.

Every man in that theater is on The club payroll.

And by The Club, I mean… me.

I own the club. This one, and two dozen more scattered all across the world.

The auctioneer. The announcer. The security team. The fluffers who bathed her.

I own all of them.

Soon I'll own her.

"Bidding begins at one hundred thousand dollars."

The number was my idea. High enough to make her feel valuable. Low enough that she won't question why someone would pay more.

A man in the third row raises his paddle.

"One hundred thousand."

Another paddle. "One hundred ten."

"One hundred twenty."

The bids climb in increments I designed. Not too fast—that would seem suspicious. Not too slow—I want her to feel wanted.

Worth fighting over.

"One hundred forty."

"One hundred fifty."

I shift in my chair, adjust the growing pressure of my engorged cock. Watching her on those screens—the confusion and shame warring across her face as strangers pretend to compete for her—is better than any scene I've ever witnessed.

She has no idea.

No idea that the confident girl who mocked her in the waiting room was hired specifically to make Scarletta feel inadequate. No idea that the nervous girl's story about the pre-arranged rape fantasy was designed to plant seeds of doubt.

No idea that every camera angle, every humiliation, every moment of her preparation was orchestrated by me.

"One hundred fifty-seven thousand dollars."

The final bid. Pre-arranged.

Scarletta doesn't know just how thorough I am… yet.

She will.

"Sold. Lot Number Twelve to Buyer Number Seven for one hundred fifty-seven thousand dollars."

Scarletta's knees buckle slightly. She catches herself.

The announcer's voice turns professional. Courteous.

"Miss Desmond, please exit stage left. Your experience starts now."

She picks up the white robe, wraps it around herself with shaking hands, and walks off the platform on unsteady legs.

I drain the rest of my whiskey, set the tumbler aside, and stand.

The monitors show her being led down a hallway. Into a private room. The severe woman with the clipboard speaks to her but I've muted the audio.

Don't need to hear it. I know what she's saying.

Your buyer has requested immediate transfer. You'll be transported to his location now. The contract terms have already begun. This is how he wants you presented...

I cross the control room to the floor-to-ceiling windows overlooking the helipad.

It's a beautiful morning. Nearly noon. Twelve hours ago, she had no idea.

Five minutes from now, her understanding will begin.

She'll arrive terrified.

Perfect.

I turn toward the full-length mirror mounted on the opposite wall and study myself. Black boxer briefs cover my raging hard on, bare everywhere else. Ink covers my torso, arms, thighs, back. Every piece of art depicts the same thing.

A woman in submission. Bound, choked, fucked, eaten, displayed by a man in a black ski mask.

Every woman's face, the same face. Wearing an expression between fear and ecstasy.

I commissioned these pieces over the course of many years, one by one, each session lasting hours under the needle. This face of this woman invaded my dreams every single night—the curve of her jaw, the vulnerable slope of her neck, the way her lips would part in surrender.

A fantasy woman I was convinced existed only in my

subconscious, some amalgamation of desire I'd never find in flesh and blood.

And then... I saw her writing.

Six months ago. A random link on DarkDesires forum. "Captive" by ScarletSins.

First paragraph and I knew. The voice. The darkness. I read every story she had at the time over the course of three days. Read every comment she'd ever left. Every response. Every fragment of herself she'd scattered across that forum.

I read all her most secret, filthy desires. Things she'd never tell another living soul. Things she was ashamed of craving.

I didn't know what she looked like then. Didn't have a name, an address, a face.

I just knew it was her.

It wasn't until after hiring a private investigator to trace her digital breadcrumbs that I came up with her real name.

Scarletta Mae Desmond.

When I saw photos of her face for the first time from socials, my heart stopped.

I *knew* it was her. But now I had proof. *Her* face, *the* face. Perfectly matching the woman inked on my body.

It's not a coincidence.

I don't believe in coincidences.

It's fate.

She's mine. She's always been mine. And the tattoos prove it—proof written in ink and pain across every inch of my skin years before I knew she existed in reality.

Immediately, I put cameras in her apartment. I hired a team that specialized in corporate espionage. They had her place wired in under twenty minutes. Bedroom. Bathroom. Living room. Kitchen. Multiple separate feeds streaming directly to encrypted servers I'd set up specifically for this purpose.

Her car came next. GPS tracker installed during an oil change—I sent her a coupon for a free service, used a shell company that looked legitimate enough she didn't question it.

Then her digital life. Keylogger on her laptop that captured every single stroke. Backdoor access to her phone that mirrored every text, every call, every app she opened. Her passwords. Her browsing history. The files she thought she'd deleted.

I became addicted to watching her exist.

Tonight, I become the man inked on my skin. The man in the black ski mask who binds, chokes, fucks, eats, and displays her.

No face. No identity. Just power.

When I'm in my Tom Ford suits, not a single tattoo shows. High collars. Long sleeves. Perfectly tailored to hide everything.

My business associates see wealth and control.

My employees see discipline and competence.

Nobody sees me.

Nobody except the ones who earn it.

And now… Scarletta.

I grab the black ski mask from the table beside the mirror. Pull it over my head. Adjust the eye holes.

The man in the ink stares back at me.

Faceless. Dangerous. Exactly like her darkest fantasy.

Through the window, the helicopter appears in the distance. A black dot silhouetted against the mid-day sun pouring through gray clouds like a delivery from Heaven.

My cock throbs. I press my palm against it through the fabric, applying pressure, controlling the urge to stroke.

Not yet.

Soon.

The helicopter descends toward the illuminated pad. Lands. Rotors still spinning.

The pilot exits first. His movements are crisp, efficient— he's done this before. He circles around to the rear passenger door. Opens it. Reaches inside with one gloved hand extended.

And there she is.

Scarletta.

The external cameras feed to monitors behind me but I stay at the window, watching with my own eyes as she's guided across the heated concrete path toward the cabin's front entrance.

She's naked.

Barefoot.

Blindfolded.

Hands cuffed behind her back.

Tears stream down her face, catching the light from refracted sunbeams.

She's crying.

Not sobbing. Not hysterical. Just silent tears rolling down her cheeks while she walks barefoot across concrete she can't see, being delivered to a man she hasn't met.

My chest tightens with desire and possession.

She's mine now.

I turn to the monitors as the pilot guides her to the front door. Positions her precisely where I instructed—facing the camera mounted above the entrance.

Staring directly at the lens.

She can't see it through the blindfold but I can see her.

Trying so fucking hard to be brave.

Trying and failing.

The pilot steps back. Nods once toward the camera. Acknowledges me watching.

I make her wait.

The helicopter noise fades.

I make her wait.

She's alone.

Naked, bound, blindfolded, standing on my doorstep.

I make her wait.

I cross the room. Down the hallway. My bare feet silent on hardwood floors.

Reach the front door.

She's three feet away on the other side. I can see her on the monitor mounted beside the doorframe—another angle, closer than the external camera.

Her chest rising and falling too fast. Hyperventilating.

Lips moving. Whispering something to herself.

I unmute the audio.

"—okay it's okay you're okay this is what you wanted this is—"

Lying to herself.

Trying to believe this is just an intense scene. Just a fantasy come true. Just a rich man who paid a lot of money for a willing participant.

She has no idea what I've done.

What I'm going to do.

I turn the handle.

Open the door.

Cold air rushes in. She gasps, flinches backward, nearly loses her balance without her hands to catch herself.

I catch her instead.

Grip her upper arms. Steady her.

She freezes.

"Please," she whispers.

I don't answer.

Pull her forward. Over the threshold. Into my cabin.

Kick the door shut behind her.

The lock engages with a heavy click that makes her jerk in my grip.

"Please I—I don't—"

I spin her around. Press her back against the closed door.

She's shorter than I expected. Top of her head barely reaches my collarbone.

Fragile.

Breakable.

Mine.

I lean close. Put my mouth beside her ear.

"Welcome home, Scarletta."

Her breathing is ragged. Fast, shallow gasps that make her chest heave against the door. She's trying to control it and failing.

I love that she's failing.

I stand behind her, close enough that my chest brushes her bare back with each breath she takes. She flinches at the contact but has nowhere to go—door behind her, me in front, hands cuffed and useless.

Trapped.

She knows it.

I reach up slowly, deliberately, and touch her cheek with two fingers. Gentle. Almost tender.

She freezes.

The contradiction destroys her. I can feel it in the way her body locks up, confusion warring with fear. Rough treatment she could categorize. Fight or flight. Simple equations.

But this softness wrapped around absolute control... she has no framework for it.

I trace the line of her jaw with my fingertips, feeling the tension thrumming beneath her skin. Her pulse hammers visibly in her throat—fast, frantic, beautiful.

"Please," she whispers again.

I don't answer.

Instead, I lean in closer, bringing my mouth to the curve where her neck meets her shoulder. I press my lips there. Not a bite. Not rough. Just a kiss.

She shudders.

Her body betrays her immediately—nipples hardening, goosebumps spreading across her arms, thighs pressing together reflexively.

Arousal coded as terror.

Or terror coded as arousal.

With her, there's no difference.

I move my mouth to her ear, close enough that my breath ghosts across her skin when I speak.

"'I am kneeling,'" I whisper, quoting her own words back to her. "'Thighs spread exactly shoulder-width apart. Spine straight. Shoulders back. Hands palm-up on my thighs where he can see I'm not hiding anything.'"

She goes rigid.

Recognizes the passage instantly.

I Am Your Perfect Slave. Chapter fourteen. Raven reciting her Dom's rules after months of training. The chapter where she finally stops fighting and surrenders completely.

Her favorite scene in her favorite story.

I hacked her laptop, read her notes folder. Found the document titled "favorite scenes to reread when I need—" and she'd never finished the sentence.

But I knew what she meant.

When I need to touch myself.

I continue, my voice low and steady against her ear. "'Chin level. Eyes down unless he commands otherwise. I don't speak unless spoken to. I don't move unless given permission. I don't come unless he allows it.'"

Scarletta's breathing stutters. Stops entirely for three seconds.

Then resumes, faster than before.

"'I am his to use. His to display. His to discipline. His to reward. I exist for his pleasure and mine only matters when he decides it matters.'"

Her legs tremble. I can feel it through the contact between us.

"'I was weak before. I fought him. Questioned him. Made him prove himself over and over because I was too afraid to believe he could handle all of me.'"

A tiny sound escapes her throat. Almost a whimper.

Almost.

"'But I'm not afraid anymore. I don't need to test him. I don't need to push. I know what I am now. What I've always been.'"

I pause. Let the silence stretch. Let her remember the final line.

Then I deliver it.

"'I am his perfect slave.'"

She breaks.

Not loudly. Not dramatically.

Just a sharp inhale followed by a shaky exhale that sounds suspiciously wet.

She's crying again.

I lift my hand from her jaw and cup her face, my palm catching the tears sliding down her cheek beneath the blindfold. My thumb strokes across her skin—once, twice—wiping away the evidence of her reaction.

"You already know how to be perfect for me," I murmur, shifting my other hand down to palm her breast. Heavy. Soft. Nipple hard against my touch. "Don't you, Scarletta?"

She doesn't answer.

Can't answer.

I squeeze gently, rolling her nipple between my thumb and forefinger. Not rough. Just enough pressure to make her gasp.

"You practiced for months. Writing out every rule. Every position. Every response."

I release her breast and trail my hand down her stomach. She sucks in air, muscles contracting beneath my touch. I slowly turn her around, push her ever so slightly into the door until her cheek is pressed flat.

"You taught yourself how to kneel. How to wait. How to surrender."

My hand moves lower. Over her hip. Down to where her hands are cuffed behind her back.

I find her wrists. Grip them. Pull them forward—not hard, just insistent—until her bound hands are pressed against the front of my boxer briefs.

Against my cock.

Thick. Hard. Straining against the fabric.

She makes a choked sound and tries to pull away.

I hold her hands in place.

"Feel that?" I ask, my voice dropping lower. "That's what you do to me. Your words. Your stories. Your perfect, filthy mind."

Her fingers twitch against me. Uncertain. Trembling.

I rock my hips forward slightly, grinding my erection into her restrained palms.

"You wrote all the rules, Scarletta," I tell her, my mouth still against her ear. "You already know exactly how to be my perfect slave."

Her breathing fractures. Ragged. Desperate.

"I didn't—" she starts, voice breaking. "I didn't mean—"

"*Yes, you did.*"

I press harder, forcing her hands flat against my cock. She can feel every inch of it now. The length. The heat. The evidence of how badly I want her.

"You meant every word. Every scene. Every fantasy you wrote at three in the morning when you couldn't sleep because you were too wet to think straight."

A sob catches in her throat.

"You wrote it because you needed to see it. Needed to know what it would feel like to be completely owned by someone who understands you."

I release one of her wrists and bring my hand back up to her breast, kneading roughly this time. She arches involuntarily into the touch.

"Someone who's read everything you've ever written. Every confession. Every shameful desire you thought you could hide behind a screen name."

Her cuffed hands are still pressed against my cock. I can feel her pulse through her wrists—racing, frantic.

"You wanted someone who'd take control so you didn't have to make choices. Who'd force you to admit what you need so you didn't have to volunteer it."

I pinch her nipple hard.

She cries out.

"You wanted someone who'd make you his perfect slave."

I release her completely and step back.

She sways without my support, catching herself against the door with her shoulder, pressing her forehead against the wood.

I move close again, my front to her back. My cock fits perfectly against the curve of her ass. I let her feel it. Let her understand exactly how hard I am.

How much I want this.

How much I want *her*.

"You wrote a scene in Chapter Nine of *Chained to the Master's Bed*," I say conversationally, as if we're discussing the weather. "Where Gabriel makes Gloria recite all the ways she wants to be used while he edges her for an hour."

Scarletta whimpers.

"Do you remember that scene?"

Silence.

I reach around and grip her throat. Not choking. Just holding. Fingers pressed against her pulse points.

"I asked you a question."

"Yes," she gasps. "Yes, I remember."

"Good."

I release her throat and trail my hand down between her breasts, over her stomach, stopping just above her pussy.

"In that scene, Gloria had to tell Gabriel every filthy thing she fantasized about. Every degrading act she craved. And if she lied—if she held anything back—he'd start over from the beginning. Setting the timer for another hour. Setting her up to succeed."

My fingers dip lower. Brush against her clit.

She jerks like I've electrocuted her.

"By the end," I continue, circling her clit with light, teasing pressure, "she was begging him to let her confess. Begging to tell him her darkest secrets because keeping them inside was worse than the shame of saying them out loud."

Scarletta's hips tilt forward, seeking more pressure.

I pull my hand away.

"That's what I'm going to do to you," I tell her. "I'm going to make you confess every fantasy you've ever had. Every story you've written. Every scene that made you wet when you typed it."

I press my cock harder against her ass.

"And you're going to tell me the truth. Because you already know the rules. You wrote them."

She's shaking so hard I can feel it through the contact between us.

Perfect.

Scared.

Aroused.

Confused.

Exactly where I need her.

I step back again, putting space between us.

"Stay there," I order. "Don't move."

I cross the room to the leather chair positioned ten feet from the door. Sit. Spread my legs. Rest my hands on the armrests.

Watch her.

Blindfolded, cuffed, naked, pressed against my front door like she's afraid her legs will give out if she steps away.

She doesn't know I'm watching.

Can't see me.

But she can *feel* my eyes on her.

I let the silence stretch. Twenty seconds. Thirty.

Her breathing slows slightly. Not calm—just exhausted from the adrenaline crash.

"What's your safeword, Scarletta?" I ask.

She flinches at the sound of my voice coming from a different location.

"I—" She swallows. "Red."

That came right out of her stories. It's always red. "And if you can't speak?"

"Three taps."

"Good. Those are the only two things that will make me stop. Use them if you need to."

I pause.

"But you won't."

She makes a small, desperate sound.

"You won't use your safeword because you've been fantasizing about this for years. You don't want gentle. You want *real*."

I lean forward slightly in the chair.

"You want someone who'll push you past every limit you thought you had. Who'll make you cry, and beg, and break. Who'll fuck the shame right out of you until you can't remember why you were ever embarrassed."

Her knees buckle. She catches herself, head against the door.

"And then," I continue, my voice dropping to barely above a whisper, "you want someone who'll hold you afterward. Who'll tell you that you're perfect exactly as you are. That your darkness doesn't make you broken—it makes you *mine*."

A sob tears out of her.

Raw. Uncontrolled.

There it is.

The truth she's been hiding from herself.

I stand. Cross the room. Stop directly behind her.

"You wrote yourself a roadmap, Scarletta," I murmur

against her ear. "Every story. Every scene. Every filthy confession your characters made to their Doms so they could be shaped into something perfect."

I grip her hips.

"Now you're going to live it."

She's crying openly now. Silent tears streaming down her face, soaking the blindfold.

I turn her around to face me. Cup her face in both hands.

"But I need you to understand something very important."

I lean close. So close my lips brush hers when I speak.

"You are *already* perfect."

CHAPTER 11
SCARLETTA

You are already perfect.

His words sting me for some reason. It's… I can't explain the feeling.

It's almost invasive, this *seeing* me.

Almost mean.

I'm already perfect?

I'm not perfect. Not even close. I don't shower. I don't work. I sleep in blanket forts—

"You will confess every thought you just had out loud. *Now.*"

His command is so absolute, I whimper.

Fuck!

Fuck!

I know better! I mean, he's right I wrote the damn rules, over and over again, story after story, the same fucking rules —and this was *always* rule number one!

You will never hide your thoughts from me!

"Now, Scarletta. And if you lie, I'll know. Do you know what your punishment will be?"

I want to say no, but it's not true. I know. Because again,

I'm the one who wrote this fucking scene! "You'll stop touching me."

"I'll stop touching you." His voice is quiet. Matter-of-fact. Like he's explaining the weather. His fingertip—just one finger—trails down my front. Right over the peak of my nipple. It pauses there...

Oh god.

He squeezes it. Gentle at first. Then he twists.

I gasp—no, I fucking *choke* on air—and my pussy clenches so hard I nearly come. Right there. Just from that. My thighs go slick and I can feel it, the wetness spreading, humiliating, impossible to hide.

That's how hard my body reacts to his expert touch.

Expert.

Jesus Christ, Scarletta. *Expert*? What are you, writing purple prose in your head while a stranger twists your nipple?

But it's true. He knows exactly how much pressure. Exactly when to release. Exactly how to make my body betray every single shred of dignity I'm clinging to.

"Is this what you want, Scarletta?"

His voice is closer now. Right against my ear. His breath is warm and I can smell whiskey and something sharper—mint maybe—and underneath that, something male, and clean, and fuck, I shouldn't be cataloging his *scent* like some kind of—

"To fake your way through this amazing experience?"

Amazing.

He called this *amazing*.

I'm naked. Blindfolded. Handcuffed. Standing in a stranger's house after being sold at an auction I didn't know was fake. My nipple is still throbbing where he twisted it, and my clit is screaming, and I haven't been touched—really *touched*—in two years and he thinks I'm going to *fake* this?

"Because if so, get the fuck out."

My stomach drops.

No.

"I'm not interested in anything other than reality."

Reality.

Reality is I signed a contract for forty-four thousand dollars that I desperately need. Reality is I filled out a questionnaire admitting every sick fantasy I've ever had and this man—whoever he is—read every word of those sick fantasies and is now holding me accountable for desires I can barely admit to myself.

Reality is I *want* this.

God, I want this so much it hurts.

But he's asking me to say it out loud. To confess what I just thought. To strip away the last protective layer between who I pretend to be and who I actually am.

"I—"

My voice cracks.

Pathetic.

Start again.

"I don't want to fake it."

The words come out small. Ashamed. Exactly like I sound in real life when I'm trying to tell someone what I need and failing spectacularly because I'm fundamentally broken at human interaction.

His finger moves. Trails down from my nipple to my ribs. My stomach. He's going lower and my breath hitches because I know where he's going, and I'm so wet it's obscene, and he's going to *feel* it and know exactly how desperate I am.

"Then *don't*."

Two words. That's it.

Don't fake it.

Like it's that simple. Like I haven't spent my entire adult life pretending to be normal, pretending I don't think about captivity, and surrender, and being owned by someone who sees through all my bullshit.

His hand stops just above my mound. Resting there. Not touching anything important. Just *there*. A threat and a promise.

"Confess what you thought when I called you perfect."

No.

Please no.

I can't—

"*Now*, Scarletta."

My name in his mouth. The command in his voice. The weight of his palm against my lower belly, so close to where I'm throbbing and aching and—

"I thought—" I swallow. "I thought you were wrong."

Silence.

His hand doesn't move. Doesn't pull away. Just waits.

I'm supposed to keep going. He wants more. He wants the full thought, the complete confession, every ugly detail of my internal monologue.

"I thought I'm not perfect. I'm—I don't shower enough. I don't work. I live in blanket forts. I—"

Oh god, this is humiliating.

"I write erotica instead of paying rent. I'm two years behind on laundry. I eat cereal for dinner and sometimes I don't eat at all because I forget when I'm writing and—"

I'm spiraling. I can hear it. The self-flagellation, the litany of failures, the desperate need to prove to him that he's wrong about me so he can leave before I get attached.

Before I ruin this like I ruin everything.

"And?" His voice is still calm. Patient. "What else did you think?"

What else?

I thought—

Fuck.

"I thought it felt invasive. The way you see me. It felt... almost mean."

The confession hangs in the air between us.

Almost mean.

Jesus, Scarletta. You just told a dominant stranger who bought you at auction that his *seeing you* feels mean. Great strategy. Really excellent communication skills. This is definitely how you keep someone interested.

His hand moves.

Lower.

I stop breathing.

His fingers slide through my folds—no warning, no teasing—and I cry out. Actually *cry out* like some kind of—

"You're dripping."

Two words. Factual. Devastating.

I am. I know I am. I can feel it running down my thighs and it's shameful and obvious and—

"Your body doesn't think I'm mean, Scarletta. Your body knows exactly what it wants."

His fingers circle my clit. Once. Twice. Light pressure. Barely anything.

I whimper.

Actual whimpering. Like a dog.

Editorial note: You sound pathetic. You *are* pathetic.

"But your mind—" His fingers press harder. "Your mind wants to protect you. It wants to convince you that being seen is dangerous. That wanting this makes you broken."

How does he—

"Doesn't it?"

His question cuts through everything. All my defenses. All my careful pretending.

"Yes." The word is barely a whisper.

"Louder."

"Yes!" It comes out desperate. Broken. "Yes, I think wanting this makes me broken. I think—I think there's something wrong with me. I think normal people don't fantasize about being owned and controlled and—and watched without consent and—"

His fingers keep moving, so I stop. feeling it. Wanting it. Enjoying it.

"And you think if I really see you—all of you—I'll realize you're damaged goods."

It's not a question.

He's quoting me. My own words from the questionnaire. The section about shame.

Damaged goods.

That's what Derek called me. When I used my safeword. When he ignored it and kept going anyway and then told me I was bad at this, that I didn't know what I really wanted.

"Your ex was wrong."

My breath catches.

He knows about Derek?

"You're not damaged. You're not broken. You're exactly what I want. But you need to stop lying to yourself about what you are."

His fingers slide inside me. Two of them. Deep.

I gasp and my hips buck forward and it's too much and not enough and—

"What are you, Scarletta?"

I don't know. I don't know what answer he wants.

"I—"

"Say it. The thing you're most afraid of. The truth you hide behind your stories."

No.

Please.

"I'm a—" My voice breaks. "I'm a submissive. I'm—I want to be owned. I want someone to see all the dark parts and want me anyway and—"

His fingers curl inside me. Finding that spot. The one that makes my vision white out.

"And?"

"And I'm terrified!" The words explode out of me. "I'm terrified you'll see everything and leave anyway because I'm too much, and not enough, and I ruin everything I touch and—"

He pulls his fingers out.

The loss is devastating.

I actually sob.

"Good girl."

I don't even know how to respond to that. Good girl? I mean, I understand why he's saying it and what it's supposed to convey—I'm his plaything, his little sub, his, his, his to command and control. To collar, to bind, to choke, to fuck, to eat, to display. It's simultaneously degrading and affectionate, but—

I let out a breath. A sob comes with it. Because he's no longer in front of me. Where did he go?

I listen. Silent.

Silence.

"Hello?"

"Do you have a question for me?"

"What?" He's across the room again.

"Don't you want to ask how I know about Derek?"

My brain stutters over the name. How does this stranger know about Derek?

"Um... OK. How do you—"

"Because I killed him, Scarletta. I killed him."

The words don't land right.

I mean, I hear them. The syllables make sense individually. *I. Killed. Him.* Three words. Subject, verb, object. Basic sentence structure.

But my brain... buffers.

Like a video that won't load. Like my laptop when I have too many tabs open and everything freezes.

Did this man just say he killed my ex-boyfriend?

That's not—

That can't be—

"Don't you want to know *how* I killed him, Scarletta?"

His voice is closer now. When did he move?

"Don't you wanna know how Derek died? It's a pretty fun story…"

Fun.

He said *fun.*

I'm standing here naked, blindfolded, handcuffed, my pussy still throbbing from where his fingers were inside me thirty seconds ago, and this man—this stranger who bought me at an auction—just told me he *killed* my ex-boyfriend and called it a *fun story.*

This is—

I need to—

"I don't—" My voice sounds wrong. Distant. Like it's coming from someone else's mouth. "You didn't—"

"He called you a selfish bitch when you used your safeword. Told you that you didn't know what you really wanted. That you were bad at this."

No no no no—

"He kept going. Even after you said red. Even after you were crying. He fucked you anyway because his pleasure mattered more than your consent."

Stop.

Please stop.

"And when he was done, he told you the problem was you. That normal women don't need safewords. That if you really loved him, you'd want to please him however he wanted."

I'm shaking.

Full-body tremors. My teeth begin to chatter.

"How—" I can barely form words. "How do you know that? I never told anyone. I never—"

"I know everything about you, Scarletta. Everything you've written. Everything you've thought. Everything that's ever been done to you."

His hand touches my face. Gentle. Wrong.

I flinch.

"I cut off his fingers first. One by one. Starting with his right pinkie. He screamed a lot. Begged. Promised he'd do anything if I let him go."

I'm going to vomit.

I'm going to vomit or pass out or—

"Then I moved to more... sensitive areas. The parts of his body he used to violate your consent."

His thumb strokes my cheekbone. Tender. Horrifying.

"I wanted him to understand what it felt like. To say no and have someone ignore you. To beg for it to stop and have someone keep going anyway."

This is a nightmare.

This has to be a nightmare.

Wake up wake up wake up—

"And when I was done—when he'd suffered enough to balance the scales—I dismembered him. Burned the pieces. Scattered the ashes where no one will ever find them."

The room tilts.

I'm falling except I'm not moving and—

I sink. Down. Down. Until I'm kneeling on cold hardwood floor, still blindfolded, still handcuffed, still naked.

Still here.

With a man who just confessed to murder.

"You're insane." The words come out flat. Disconnected. "You're fucking insane and I need to—I need to leave. I need to—"

"Do you?"

His voice is right above me now. He's standing over me.

"Do you really want to leave, Scarletta? Or do you want to how I knew about him."

I don't want to know.

I don't want to know anything.

I want to go back to my apartment. Back to my blanket

fort. Back to the moment before I clicked that link and entered this nightmare.

"I've been watching you for six months, Scarletta. Reading everything you write. Learning who you are. And when I found out what Derek did to you—"

His hand touches my hair. Strokes it.

"I couldn't let him keep breathing. Not when he'd touched something that belongs to me."

Belongs to me.

"I don't belong to you." My voice shakes. "You don't even know me."

"Don't I?"

The question is almost gentle.

"I know you eat Lucky Charms for dinner standing at your kitchen counter because sitting at a table alone makes you feel pathetic. I know you wear your father's hoodie when you write because it makes you feel safe. I know you haven't done laundry in two weeks and you've been rewearing your leggings because you can't seem to care about anything but your sex fantasies."

Stop.

"I know you write your darkest fantasies at three AM when you can't sleep because the silence in your apartment gets too loud. I know you touch yourself while you write but sometimes you deny yourself orgasms because somewhere in your broken brain, you think you don't deserve pleasure unless someone gives you permission."

How—

"I know Derek fucked up your relationship with your own desire. Made you think wanting to submit made you damaged. Made you think your fantasies were proof of your brokenness."

His fingers tilt my chin up. Forcing me to face where I think he's standing even though I can't see.

"And I know that right now—even as terrified as you are

—part of you is wet because I killed the man who hurt you. Part of you is aroused because someone finally saw what he did and decided he needed to pay for it."

"That's not—"

"Isn't it?"

His thumb presses against my lower lip.

"Your body doesn't lie, Scarletta. Your pussy doesn't lie. You can tell yourself you're horrified. You can convince yourself this is wrong. But your body knows the truth."

I'm shaking harder now.

Uncontrollable convulsions.

"You write about this. Over and over. Men who kill for their women. Men who destroy anyone who threatens what's theirs. You write about it because you crave it. Because somewhere deep in your psyche, you want to be valuable enough that someone would burn the world down to protect you."

No.

That's fiction. That's fantasy. That's not—

"And now you have it. A man who killed for you. A man who'll do worse if anyone ever hurts you again."

His voice drops lower.

"So tell me, Scarletta. Do you really want to leave? Do you really want to go back to your empty apartment, and your blanket fort, and your stories about men who don't exist?"

Silence.

I can't speak.

Can't think.

Can't—

"Or do you want to stay here with the monster you've been writing about your entire adult life?"

CHAPTER 12
CALEB

Go. Or Stay.

These are her choices. It's just that simple.

But to a girl like Scarletta, nothing about sex is simple. She's got a dark side. A dark side she's been hiding her whole life. A dabble here with that sick fuck, Derek. A dabble there, writing down her fantasies isn't *nothing*. But it's still a fantasy.

She's breathing very hard now. Shaking like a little bird. Teeth chattering, even though it's seventy-two degrees in the foyer. Whimpering like a puppy. Completely lost all her composure.

"I'm gonna need an answer, little slut."

She gasps at the insult. Except, it's not an insult.

I pet her cheek. "My good little slut, I should say. If you *want* to be. If you're ready."

"Ready for what?" she asks.

My fingers are playing with her lips now—soft, full, slightly parted as she struggles to catch her breath. I'm picturing them doing all kinds of things to my cock. Wrapped around it. Stretched wide. Those perfect lips forming a perfect O as I push inside. The visual alone makes my dick throb against my zipper.

"To become the woman you've always wanted to be," I tell her, my voice low and measured. "To free yourself from the shame that's been eating you alive for years. To not only understand your desires—those dark, twisted, beautiful desires you've been pouring into your stories—but to actually experience them. To live them. That's what I can give you, Scarletta. That's what this night is really about."

I pause, letting that sink in, watching her pupils dilate even further.

"In addition to the forty-four thousand dollars, that is." I let my thumb drag across her bottom lip, just enough pressure to feel how soft it is. "Because if you leave right now, if you walk out that door, you don't get paid. Not a single fucking cent. I'm not going to force you to stay here with me —that would defeat the entire purpose. But you need to fully understand exactly what you're walking away from if you go."

I lean in closer, so close I can feel the heat radiating off her flushed skin. "If you want the money, you need to earn it. Every. Single. Dollar."

"What do you want me to do?" Her voice trembles, barely a whisper.

I let out a low scoff, sharp and dismissive. "It's not what I want you to do, my little slut. It's what you want *me* to do." I watch her chest rise and fall in rapid succession. "That's why you checked those boxes, isn't it? Why your hand probably shook when you filled out that form, heart pounding, pussy getting wet as you imagined each scenario playing out in vivid, excruciating detail."

She sucks in a long, shuddering breath, and I can hear the war playing out in her head—the part of her that wants to deny it battling with the part that's desperate for this.

"You want me to play with you," I continue, my voice dropping lower, more intimate. "Tease your pussy with toys until you're begging. Spank you until you can't sit comfortably for days. Heavy bondage—rope, leather, steel, whatever strikes my fancy—until you can't move a single inch without my permission." I pause, letting each word sink in. "But that's not even the best part, is it?"

Her breathing hitches.

"You want me to degrade you too. Control you. Everything. What you eat, when you eat it. When you're allowed to piss. Every sexual act, down to the smallest detail. You want me to fuck with your head, treat you like furniture when the mood strikes, make you confess your sickest, darkest, most disturbing desires—the ones you've never told another living soul. The ones that make you question if there's something fundamentally broken inside you."

I reach up quickly, my hand fisting in her hair with enough force to make her gasp. Then, slowly—agonizingly slowly—I pull her head back until she's looking straight up at the ceiling, her throat exposed, vulnerable, the long line of her neck a pale offering in the dim light.

I lean in close to that exposed flesh, my lips barely grazing the sensitive skin just below her ear, and whisper, "Just so we're perfectly clear, you already gave me permission to do all of these things, Scarletta. Every single one. This isn't a negotiation. I've bought these permissions. The transaction is complete. It's done." I let my breath ghost across her skin, feeling her shiver. "And if you stay—when you stay—all of that is going to happen. Not some of it. Not the parts you think you can handle. All. Of. It."

A single tear appears from a gap in her blindfold. It slides down her cheek, catching the dim light as it traces a path along the curve of her cheekbone.

I lean in slowly, deliberately, and press my lips to it— tasting salt and fear and surrender all at once. The intimacy of the gesture is at complete odds with the brutality of what I've just promised her, and I can feel her breathing stutter in response.

"It's okay," I murmur against her skin. "It's okay to be scared, my good little slut. It's completely normal. Natural, even." I pause, letting that sink in. "You *should* be scared. You don't know me—not really. For all you know, I could be someone truly evil. Someone who would break you and leave you in pieces." My thumb traces the wet track the tear left behind. "Being afraid right now? That's your job."

I lean in again, this time pressing my lips to the exposed column of her throat where her pulse hammers wildly against my mouth. I let my lips drift lower, trailing down to the curve of her shoulder, taking my time, savoring every tremor, every stuttered breath. I register the quick, sharp intake of air when my teeth graze her collarbone. I notice the way her nipples have drawn up into tight, hard points—her body responding even as her mind tries to process the enormity of what she's agreed to.

"My job..." I continue, my voice a low rumble against her skin, "is to keep you afraid until you don't care anymore. Until the pleasure I deliver is so delicious, so perfectly overwhelming, so goddamn *heavenly*—that it completely overpowers your fear. Your pain. Your doubt. Until all that exists between us is—*us*."

She bites down on her quivering lower lip, her chest rising and falling rapidly, each breath shallow and labored. "What... what if I can't take it?" The words tumble out in a rush, barely more than a whisper. A sob catches in her throat, and her whole body shudders with it. "What if I'm no good at this? What if I disappoint you? What if—"

"Shhhhh." I press a single fingertip to her lips, silencing the spiral before it can drag her down further. The touch is gentle, but the command behind it is absolute. "That's not going to happen, Scarletta." I hold her head, refusing to let her look down. "Because if you're not good at it—if you struggle, if you stumble, if you break—it's not your fault, darling. It's mine."

She sucks in three quick, desperate breaths through her nose, her ribcage expanding and contracting like a bird trapped against glass. She's teetering on the edge of hyperventilation, her pupils dilating with panic. "What?" The word comes out strangled, disbelieving.

"That's right, my sweet slut." I stroke her cheek with the backs of my knuckles, slow and soothing, grounding her. "Your job—your *only* job—is to show up for me. To do everything I tell you to do. Answer every question I ask you, truthfully and without hesitation. Hold any position I put you in, for as long as I demand it—"

"But what if *I can't*?" The interruption bursts from her, raw and ragged. Desperate for reassurance, terrified of the answer.

"Then you fail." I cup her cheek again, my thumb brushing away a fresh tear that's escaped the blindfold. My voice is calm, matter-of-fact, as if we're discussing something mundane.

"Failing—when you're doing it with me, at least—is part of the experience, Scarletta. If you can't hold the position I've put you in, if your muscles give out, if you fall apart completely... well, that's information. That's me learning your limits."

I lean in closer, my breath ghosting across her lips. "I come over. I reposition you. I adjust my expectations. I make you try again. I encourage you when you need it. I hold you up when you're trembling. I help you do what I'm asking of you. And then—*then*—I reward you for trying."

My hand slides down from her face, trailing over the curve of her throat, between her breasts, across the soft plane of her stomach. She's trembling harder now, her breath coming in shallow pants. When my fingers reach her pussy, I don't hesitate. I cup her roughly, possessively, and one finger slides easily between her thoroughly soaked folds. She's drenched—slick, and swollen, and *ready*.

I push inside her, slow and deliberate, feeling her inner walls clench around the intrusion. Her back arches involuntarily, a sharp gasp tearing from her throat. Her mouth falls open, eyes fluttering shut, and a low, helpless moan escapes as I crook my finger, finding that spot inside her that makes her see stars.

I finger her with purpose, curling and stroking, watching every flicker of pleasure that crosses her face. She's coming apart in my arms—hips rocking against my hand, thighs trembling, her whole body surrendering to the sensation.

Beautiful. Absolutely fucking beautiful.

Then I withdraw. Slowly. The wet sound of it obscene in the quiet cabin. Her mouth opens, confused and bereft, her pussy clenching around nothing.

Before she can protest, I bring my fingers—glistening with her arousal—to her still-open mouth and press them against her bottom lip. "Suck them," I whisper, my voice dark and edged with command. "Taste yourself. Taste how much you want this."

Her lips close over my fingers without hesitation, her tongue pressing up against the pads, licking them clean. She sucks—really sucks—hollowing her cheeks as saliva pools in her mouth, mixing with her own slick, and the sight of it—of her, so obedient, so eager—sends a bolt of heat straight to my cock.

I pull my fingers free from her mouth with a slick, wet sound that makes her whimper—needy and desperate. A thin strand of saliva connects my fingertips to her bottom lip before it breaks, glistening in the dim light.

"Good girl," I murmur, my voice rough with approval and raw desire, and I watch her eyes flutter closed, her breath hitching as the praise sinks deep into her psyche. She *needs* this—needs to be told she's doing well, needs to be acknowledged, validated, claimed. "Such a good fucking slut."

My hand moves to her hair, fingers threading through the tangled, disheveled strands with deliberate tenderness. I stroke slowly, petting her like she's something precious I've just taken possession of.

My fingers are still wet—slick with her arousal and her saliva—and I spread it through her hair without shame, marking her with the evidence of her own desperate need. The strands stick together, damp and messy, and the sight of it—of her looking so thoroughly debauched, so beautifully ruined—sends another surge of possessive heat through my chest.

She leans into my touch like a cat seeking affection, a soft, broken sound escaping her throat. Her body is pliant now, boneless and utterly surrendered when I place the palm of my hand across her throat. I can feel the last vestiges of her resistance melting away under my touch.

I squeeze—she doesn't panic. And this just makes me harder. Instead, she sucks in a deep, deep breath and then slowly, deliberately, she lets it out. The exhale is shaky, unsteady, like she's releasing more than just air. Like she's releasing the last fragile thread of resistance she's been clinging to.

I already know what she's going to say. I can see it in the way her body has softened against mine, in the way her thighs are still parted, in the way her lips are still wet from sucking my fingers clean. She's going to stay. She was always going to stay.

But I need to hear it.

The cameras need to hear it.

I need her consent—clear, explicit, unambiguous—captured in perfect audio. Not just for the legality of it, though that matters. But because I need her to know, later, when doubt creeps in, that she chose this. That she said yes. That she wanted me.

I shift slightly, easing my grip on her throat just enough that she can speak freely. My other hand rests possessively on her hip, keeping her anchored to me. I lean in close, my lips brushing the shell of her ear, my voice low and dark and utterly serious.

"Time to answer my question, ScarletSins." I let the name roll off my tongue like a secret, like a weapon. "Will you give in to me? Keep your end of the agreement so I can keep mine?" I pause, letting the weight of the choice settle over her. "Or would you like me to send you home?"

She hesitates.

But it's not real hesitation—not the kind that matters. It's a moment for her to construct the narrative she'll tell herself later. That she doesn't have a choice. That she needs the money too desperately. That this isn't really her decision, that circumstances forced her hand, that she's a victim of her own desperation. She's going to say yes anyway, but she needs to believe the lie first. Needs to wrap herself in the fiction that this is happening *to* her rather than because she *wants* it.

It's all lies.

Self-deception at its finest.

But I don't care.

She can lie to herself all she wants—weave whatever pretty story helps her sleep at night, construct whatever justification makes her feel less culpable for the darkness she craves. As long as she never lies to *me*. As long as when I ask her a direct question, I get the truth. The rest? The mental gymnastics she performs to reconcile her desires with her self-image? That's her business.

"OK," she finally whispers, the word barely audible.

"OK?" The word comes out sharp, dangerous. I reach back and fist her hair again, harder this time, yanking her head back at an angle that exposes the full column of her throat. The movement is brutal, sudden, designed to shock.

"OK, *what*, you little fucking whore?" I don't soften my growl. Don't add the velvet coating that makes dominance palatable. Don't pretend that I'm something I'm not—something safe, something civilized, something that won't actually hurt her. "Is that how you talk to your fucking master? You know the fucking rules, slut. You wrote them, remember?"

For a moment—a beautiful, crystalline moment—she's terrified. Genuinely afraid. Her whole body goes rigid against me, her breathing stops, and I can feel the rabbit-quick flutter of her pulse against my palm. She's unable to reconcile the switch in my demeanor, the sudden shift from the man who praised her for coming to the man who's calling her a whore with real venom in his voice.

But then, over the course of several long seconds, I watch understanding bloom across her features.

We're playing now.

It's time.

The scene has begun.

I'm in character—the Master she wrote about in her stories, the dominant who doesn't ask, or negotiate, or soften his commands.

She should be in character too.

Not Scarletta, the girl who can't pay rent, and hides behind hoodies, and bites her nails until they bleed.

Not the nervous woman who flinched when she was disrobed and cuffed, who trembled in my doorway.

No.

Right now, in this moment, she needs to be the submissive she created in her stories—the one who knows her place, who understands the rules of surrender, who doesn't say "OK" to her Master like they're negotiating the terms of a fucking fast food order.

She needs to be mine completely.

That's the role she's playing now.

And if she doesn't understand that yet, I'll teach her.

But she does.

She *did* write the rules.

"Yes, Master," she says, bowing her head in a gesture of submission that looks almost instinctive. "I'm here to serve you. Please tell me what to do."

Perfect.

"Come with me." I grab her arm just above the elbow—not gently, not with care for her comfort—and start pulling her across the hardwood floor. She stumbles immediately, her bare feet sliding on the polished surface, her balance thrown by the blindfold and the cuffs.

She nearly trips, her body lurching forward. I don't stop the fall so much as drag her out of it, using my grip on her arm to keep her upright through sheer forward momentum. She recovers with a small, helpless whimper, her feet scurrying now to keep pace, hands still cuffed behind her back, eyes still blind—as I lead her toward the wide, curved stairwell that descends to my playroom.

When we reach the stairs, I stop. She's breathing hard, her chest heaving, a fine sheen of sweat already visible on her skin despite the cold air. I lean down and scoop her up without warning, cradling her in my arms like a child. The position pulls sharply on her shoulders, forcing her arms at an unnatural angle behind her back, pressing against the cuffs holding her wrists captive.

It's painful. I know it's painful. I can feel the way her muscles tense, the way her breath catches. That's precisely why I did it.

She whines—a small, animal sound of distress—and I feel the wet warmth of fresh tears soaking into the blindfold. But then we're downstairs, the temperature dropping noticeably as we descend into the basement level, and I'm striding quickly across the concrete floor toward the bondage table.

I set her down on the surface without ceremony. She gasps

at the crinkle of white paper beneath her, the clinical sound at odds with everything else about this moment.

"Lean forward," I command.

She obeys, shifting her weight, and I reach for the key I left waiting on the small stainless steel tray beside the table. The metallic *clink* of the key sliding into the lock echoes in the quiet room, followed by the distinct *snick* of the mechanism releasing. I remove the cuffs efficiently, setting them aside, and watch as she brings her arms forward with a shuddering exhale of relief.

She's processing—I can see it in the subtle shift of her expression, in the way her mouth opens slightly as if to speak. The sound of medical instruments against stainless steel is doing something to her, triggering associations she's not ready to examine. But the relief from having her shoulders released dominates everything else. As it should. She doesn't have time yet to understand where this is going.

"Lie back now," I say, my hand pressing against the small of her back to guide her down.

She complies, lowering herself onto the crinkling paper. I'm already moving to the end of the table before she's fully settled, my hands reaching for her knees, pulling her bent legs down toward the stirrups, then spreading them open.

She gasps, her whole body tensing. "What—what are we doing?"

I don't answer. Don't waste words on explanations she doesn't need. Instead, I cup the heel of her left foot in my palm and guide it firmly into the waiting stirrup, the cold metal a stark contrast against her warm skin.

"Oh, god," she moans, the sound half terror, half arousal.

I allow myself a small smile as I guide her right foot into the other stirrup, spreading her legs wide, exposing her completely.

Because she knows exactly what we're doing.

She's written this scene six times, in six different stories.

The vulnerable position, the clinical setting, the loss of control.

She knows, and the knowledge is already making her wet.

Now she just has to live it.

CHAPTER 13
SCARLETTA

The humiliation begins immediately, flooding through me in waves that make my skin prickle with shame.

Just the fact that I've written this scene—that I've sat in my blanket fort and carefully crafted every degrading detail—is enough to make my mind spiral into another pit of self-loathing.

My fingers had flown across the keyboard as I typed it out, my pulse quickening with each word, my thighs pressing together involuntarily as the scene took shape in my imagination.

What kind of sick fuck sexualizes a gynecological examination? What kind of person takes something clinical and sterile and transforms it into something twisted and arousing?

You, Scarletta. You, that's who. You're the one who thought of this. You're disgusting, you're broken, you're—

"I'm going to take your blindfold off now."

Of course he is. That's exactly how this scene goes, every single time I've written variations of it. The girl—me, I'm the girl, OK? It's me! Let's stop pretending it's some fictional character—she's always ashamed of what's happening to her body, of her reactions, of the way she's restrained and exposed.

So the Master makes her watch. Forces her to witness her own degradation, to see exactly what he's doing to her, because watching makes it worse. Makes it more real. Makes the humiliation complete.

He's right up next to me now, so close I can feel the heat radiating from his body as he presses his torso against my arm. His fingers slip behind my head with practiced efficiency—and I lift up automatically, tilting my chin to give him better access, to help... to help? *What is wrong with me?* Why am I cooperating with my own humiliation? Why does some broken part of my brain think I should make this easier for him?

But there's no time to answer that question, no time to psychoanalyze my fucked-up responses, because he pulls the blindfold away and suddenly I'm hit directly in the eyes with a stark, bright examination light.

I blink rapidly, my eyes watering from the sudden assault of brightness after the darkness. Once, twice, three times, trying to adjust to the glare. Then, finally, my vision clears enough to find his face, to look up at the man who's been touching me, who's seen every intimate part of me.

He's wearing a suit—like a tux. But he doesn't have a face. Not one I can see, anyway. Because he's wearing a black ski mask that covers everything except his eyes and mouth.

And that mouth is smiling. A slow, deliberate curve of lips that somehow manages to be both welcoming and predatory at the same time. "Hello."

"Uhh..." The sound escapes before I can stop it, barely even qualifying as a word. Just a pathetic stuttering noise that makes me sound like I've forgotten how human speech works. I stutter. Literally stutter. Over a simple greeting. Over the word 'hello'.

Jesus Christ, what is wrong with me?

"I've got your chart here, Scarletta," he says, and his voice is so perfectly professional, so clinically cool and detached, like we're actually in a real examination room and he's actually a real doctor about to discuss my actual medical history. Not... whatever the fuck this is. "I've taken a good long look at it. Read through every detail very carefully."

"Oh... uh... yes, Master." The title feels strange on my tongue, formal and subservient and absolutely surreal given the circumstances, given that I still can't see his actual face, given that I'm on my back on a gynecological exam table with my legs spread wide and everything on display.

"What do you think it says?" He asks the question like it's perfectly reasonable, like he's genuinely curious about my opinion, like we're having a normal conversation and not... *this*.

I want to sigh here. Desperately. Want to let out a long, loud, exasperated breath that conveys exactly how ridiculous this question is.

What do I *think* it says? I know exactly what it says. Every single word, every fabricated detail, every carefully constructed piece of fictional medical history.

I wrote the fucking chart.

Like, literally sat down at my computer and made a chart from scratch. Photoshopped the whole thing with a template I found online, formatted it to look official and clinical, and filled it in with every minute detail about insert-your-favorite-FMC-here-written-by-ScarletSins-who-is-really-just-Scarletta-Mae-Desmond.

He taps a blue Bic pen on the folder's edge—a slow, deliberate rhythm that makes the cheap plastic click against the manila paper.

Oh, shit.

The Bic pen.

The goddamn Bic pen.

The fucking *Bic* fucking *pen*.

Of all the objects in this room—the leather restraints, the metal stirrups, the clinical instruments arranged with surgical precision on the tray beside me—it's that worthless piece of disposable plastic that makes my breath catch. That makes heat flood my face, and chest, and lower belly, spreading through my exposed body like wildfire.

My master chuckles, a low sound that vibrates through the charged air between us. He looks at the pen in his hand, then slowly, deliberately, shifts his gaze to my face. Studies me with pale grey-blue eyes that I still can't fully see in the dim lighting but can *feel* dissecting every involuntary response.

"I see this excites you," he observes, his voice carrying that note of dark amusement that suggests he knows *exactly* why my breathing just changed, exactly what's running through my mind right now, exactly which scene from which story that cheap blue pen is calling back to.

"It's familiar, isn't it?" he asks, his voice deceptively casual. He turns the pen between his fingers—slow, methodical rotations—studying it like it's some fascinating artifact he's never encountered before. Like he hasn't read that scene a dozen times. Like he doesn't know *exactly* what this particular implement means, what it represents, what I wrote about it in excruciating, humiliating detail.

My throat feels like I've swallowed sand. I swallow hard anyway, trying to work moisture back into my mouth. Then I nod—a jerky, graceless movement that makes the restraints creak.

Then I remember. The rules. His rules. *MY* rules. No gestures without words.

"Yes, Master," I manage, the words scraping past my lips.

A pause. He's waiting. I can feel the weight of his expectation pressing down on me, patient and inexorable as gravity.

"Refresh my memory," he says finally, and there's a thread of steel beneath the silk of his tone.

This is it. This is where I die. Not from anything he does to my body, but from pure, crystallized mortification. My own words, weaponized against me.

"Scarletta?" My name cuts through the haze of panic.

"Yes, Master." Automatic now. Pavlovian.

"Recite the scene to me." He pauses, lets that command settle into my bones. Then adds, almost conversationally, "It's... one of your best."

Forty-four thousand dollars, Scarletta. The number blazes across my consciousness like a neon sign. *Forty-four fucking K. You sold this. You wrote this scene, you put it out into the world for strangers to read and touch themselves to, and now you're going to say it out loud to the man holding that pen.*

I draw in a shaking breath.

It's your scene. Your words. Just... fucking say them.

I close my eyes. Open them. The examination light burns into my retinas.

"It's from 'The Appointment,'" I whisper.

"Louder."

"It's from 'The Appointment.'" My voice cracks. "The story where—where the protagonist goes to see her gynecologist and she has this whole elaborate fantasy about him while she's in the stirrups and—"

"I didn't ask for a summary." His tone is patient. Relentless. "I asked you to recite the scene."

Oh god. Oh fuck. Oh Jesus Christ and every saint who's ever existed.

My face is on fire. My entire body is burning with shame so intense it feels physical, like my skin might actually combust from the sheer mortification of what he's asking me to do.

The thing is—the *thing* is—that scene wasn't even supposed

to be hot. It was supposed to be funny. Absurd. A satirical commentary on the way we sexualize completely inappropriate situations, the way our minds wander during mundane medical procedures, the disconnect between reality and fantasy.

Except apparently I'm shit at funny. Or maybe everyone else is shit at recognizing my brand of humor, because when I posted that story, when 'The Appointment' went live on DarkDesires, the comments section exploded. People loved it. Called it revolutionary. Said it was the hottest thing they'd ever read. That scene—the pen scene specifically—became legendary. Made ScarletSins a name people actually knew on the forum.

And now I have to recite it. Out loud. To the masked man standing between my spread legs holding the exact object I wrote about.

"I'm waiting, Scarletta."

My throat works. Words stick like broken glass.

"She's—" I start, then stop. Clear my throat. "The protagonist, her name is Sindy—"

Sindy, Scarletta, SINdy? As in ScarletSins? My god…

"Scarletta?"

"She's… she's lying on the exam table just like—just like this. Legs in stirrups. Paper gown. And Dr. Bennett walks in with a clipboard and he's younger than she expected, maybe thirty, with dark hair and these really intense eyes that make her feel exposed even before he touches her."

"Keep going."

I swallow hard. The words are burned into my memory— I've read that scene so many times, editing it, posting it, refreshing the page to watch comments roll in.

"He tells her he needs to do a routine examination and she says okay even though her heart is pounding. He sits on the rolling stool and positions himself between her legs and she's trying to think about anything else—grocery lists, work deadlines, anything—but then he touches her inner thigh to adjust her position and her mind just… goes."

The pen taps against the folder. Click. Click. Click.

"She starts imagining that he's not just doing a medical exam, that he's… studying her. That every touch is deliberate. That he's cataloging her responses. She fantasizes that he notices when she gets wet, when her breathing changes, when her thighs tremble slightly."

My voice is shaking now. I can hear it, that quiver that betrays exactly how mortified I am.

"Go on."

"He—he picks up a pen. A blue Bic pen just like—" I can't finish. Can't say 'just like the one you're holding' because that makes this too real, collapses the distance between fiction and whatever the fuck is happening to me right now.

Master taps the pen against my inner thigh. Not hard. Just enough pressure to make me flinch.

"Just like this one?"

"Yes, Master."

"Continue."

I'm going to die. Actually die. My heart will give out from pure shame and they'll find my body on this exam table and the autopsy report will list cause of death as 'humiliation-induced cardiac arrest.'

"In the fantasy, Dr. Bennett runs the pen along her inner thigh. Traces patterns with it. Circles higher and higher until he's almost touching her pussy but not quite. And Mara is losing her mind because it's just a pen, it's just a cheap plastic pen, but the way he's using it—the clinical precision, the detachment, like this is all part of the examination—makes it unbearable."

My breath is coming faster. I can feel my pulse throbbing between my legs, that treacherous wetness starting to gather again.

"He asks her questions while he does this. Medical

questions. Is she sexually active? Does she experience pain during intercourse? Does she achieve orgasm regularly? And she has to answer while he's dragging this pen across her skin, getting closer to where she's aching, where she desperately needs to be touched."

Master sits down on a rolling stool. Wheels between my legs, smiles at me under the mask. Then the pen in his hand moves. Trails along my left inner thigh, mimicking the scene I'm describing. My hips jerk involuntarily.

"What happens next?"

"He—" My voice breaks completely. "He tells her he needs to check her sensitivity. That it's a standard part of the exam. He takes the pen and he—he touches it to her clit. Just barely. Just the rounded tip of the pen pressed against her and she nearly comes right then because it's so wrong, because this isn't what pens are for, because she's in a doctor's office with her legs spread and this man is touching her with office supplies and—"

"And?"

"And she's so wet. So fucking wet that the pen slides easily, that when he starts circling her clit with it she can hear the obscene wet sounds her pussy is making, can feel herself soaking the paper on the exam table."

The pen touches my clit.

I gasp—a sharp, desperate sound that echoes in the clinical space.

"He makes notes," I continue, my voice barely above a whisper now. "In her fantasy, he's writing on the clipboard with one hand while using the pen on her clit with the other. Notes about her arousal levels, her responsiveness, the way her hips lift seeking more pressure. And the fact that he's documenting this, that he's treating her orgasm like data to be recorded, makes it even more intense."

The pen circles. Slow. Methodical. Exactly as I wrote it.

"She tries to stay quiet but she can't. Little whimpering

sounds escape and he tells her that vocalization is normal, that she shouldn't suppress her natural responses, that he needs accurate data. And that permission to make noise, to stop holding back, destroys her last bit of control."

I'm panting now. Can't help it. The pen is still moving, still circling, the cheap plastic slick with my arousal.

"He asks her to describe what she's feeling. Forces her to put words to it while he's touching her. She has to say things like 'pressure on my clitoris' and 'vaginal lubrication' and 'muscle contractions' because he wants clinical terminology, wants her to narrate her own humiliation in medical language."

"Very good," Master murmurs. "And then?"

"Then he tells her he needs an internal measurement. He caps the pen and—and he pushes it inside her. Just slides it in while she's still throbbing from the clitoral stimulation. The pen is smooth and hard and nothing like a cock or a dildo, and that wrongness makes her clench around it."

The pen at my clit disappears. I hear the click of the cap.

Oh fuck. Oh no. He wouldn't—

"Keep reciting, Scarletta."

But before I can continue, before I can form another word, I feel it—smooth plastic pressing against my opening, teasing for just a heartbeat before it slides inside me. Not just the pen, though. His finger too. One thick digit alongside the hard barrel of the pen, stretching me, filling me in a way that's so utterly wrong it short-circuits my brain.

The dual penetration makes me gasp—the clinical smoothness of the plastic contrasted with the warm, slightly rough texture of his skin. Two distinctly different sensations occupying the same intimate space.

My eyes slam shut on instinct, my body trying to retreat somewhere inside itself where this isn't happening, where I'm not being penetrated with office supplies while reciting my own filthy fantasies.

But that's cowardice. That's hiding.

I force my eyes back open. Force myself to see the scene in the mirror—my legs spread, his hand between my thighs, his expression of cool clinical interest as he watches my face for every micro-expression of response.

"Scarletta?" His voice is patient but firm. Waiting. The pen and his finger remain perfectly still inside me, a constant presence I can't ignore or forget. "You stopped. Keep reciting."

"Then he pushes the pen up—" The words come out as a strangled squeak because he's moving now, not just moving but *fingering* me. Not the gentle exploration I'd expected but actual fucking—his finger and the pen working in tandem, pumping in and out of me with purpose and intensity. Hard. Rough. The kind of rhythm that makes my thighs shake and my breath catch in my throat.

Then… something happens here. Something I wasn't prepared for. Something my body does entirely without my permission.

I'm coming.

Not the gentle build I'm used to when I touch myself alone in my apartment. Not the slow climb toward release that I can control, can edge away from, can decide when to tip over into.

This is *hard*. Harder than anything I've ever experienced before in my entire life. A detonation that starts where his finger and that goddamn pen are working inside me and radiates outward in concentric waves of sensation so intense my vision actually whites out at the edges.

I can't see. Can't hear anything except the roaring in my ears and the sounds coming out of my own mouth—high, desperate noises I don't recognize, whimpers, and gasps, and something that might be Master or might just be incoherent begging.

Can't function.

My hips are jerking against his hand, chasing more of that

unbearable pleasure even as it threatens to shatter me into pieces. My fingers have lost their grip on my thighs entirely, hands scrabbling uselessly at the leather padding beneath me. Everything in my body has narrowed to a single point of overwhelming sensation.

I'm dimly aware that I'm making a spectacle of myself. Coming undone in front of him, on his hand, penetrated by office supplies while mirrors show my degradation from every angle.

But I can't stop it.

Can't control it.

Can't do anything but *feel*.

CHAPTER 14
CALEB

The sight of Scarletta losing control is so utterly mesmerizing, so viscerally captivating, that I can't tear my eyes away from her for even a fraction of a second. She's writhing beneath my touch, her body twisting and arching against the table, those gorgeous legs of hers trembling and shaking from the force of her orgasm.

The muscles in her thighs are quivering, taut and flexed, and I can feel the aftershocks rippling through her core where my finger and the pen are still buried deep inside her slick heat.

Her knees slam together with desperate force, thighs clenching tight as her feet slip free from the stirrups entirely, heels sliding against the leather padding of the table. I don't stop fingering her—I absolutely refuse to stop, not now, not when she's this far gone.

I continue the relentless rhythm inside her, curling and stroking against that perfect spot that makes her entire body shake, even as her legs try instinctively to close against the overwhelming sensation.

My mind is working on two levels simultaneously—one part completely absorbed in the exquisite sight before me, the other part already analyzing, calculating, mentally reconfiguring this entire scene for next time.

I'm mentally kicking myself for not restraining her properly. Next time I'll use cuffs on her wrists and ankles, locked tight so she can't escape what I'm giving her. A spreader bar between her knees to keep those gorgeous thighs forced wide open, to maintain her in that vulnerable position no matter how intense it gets, no matter how desperately she wants to close her legs against the onslaught.

But then again... perhaps this wild, unrestrained display is even better precisely *because* of her freedom, because of her ability to move, and writhe, and lose control completely.

I keep going, keep pumping inside her with deliberate, measured strokes. The wet sounds are obscene in the quiet of the playroom, mixing with her ragged breathing and broken whimpers. She crests—I know she crests, I can recognize the exact moment when it happens, the way her entire body goes rigid and then suddenly relaxes, that telltale loosening of tension that signals the peak has passed.

But in the next instant, before she can even catch her breath, she's coming undone all over again.

A second orgasm crashes through her, harder than the first.

After watching her for six long months—watching her in the privacy of her studio apartment, watching her masturbate at least once a day, sometimes three or four times if she's writing something she's really into, something particularly dark or depraved that turns her on—I genuinely thought I'd seen everything.

I thought I'd catalogued every possible variation, every subtle difference in how this woman could climax. I'd watched her use her fingers, watched her grind against pillows, watched her bite her lip to stay quiet even though she was completely alone.

But she's never, ever done this before.

She's never come so hard that her entire body shook like this, never lost control so completely that she couldn't even form words.

I pump my finger and pen into her again, harder this time, curling deep and pressing with deliberate precision. I lean into the motion, using my body weight, shifting my position so I can wedge myself properly between her spread thighs. My shoulder presses against the inside of her left knee, keeping her legs forced wide apart even as her muscles tremble and try instinctively to close, to protect herself from the overwhelming intensity of what I'm doing to her.

She squirts.

Clear liquid suddenly gushes from her pussy in a hot, forceful stream. It coats my suit, my arms, some of it hits my face. The warmth of it unmistakable even through the haze of adrenaline.

More fluid pulses out of her with each continued thrust of my fingers. The sensation is shocking—visceral in a way I hadn't fully anticipated, even though I'd been deliberately working toward this exact response.

She's screaming now—broken, gasping syllables torn from her throat without thought or control. "Oh, God. Oh, my God. Oh! Oh!" The words tumble out in rapid succession, her voice cracking on each one, pitching higher with every wave of sensation that crashes through her.

There's no coherence left, no filter between what she's feeling and what she's expressing. Just raw, unfiltered reaction—primal, and desperate, and completely genuine.

Her hips buck violently against my hand, her body arching so sharply off the table, I have to quickly grab her leg to prevent her from rolling off.

I don't stop.

I keep my finger and the pen buried deep inside her, maintaining that relentless pressure against her G-spot even as her inner walls clench and pulse around me.

I place my other hand firm on her lower belly, pressing down with steady, unyielding force. I can feel everything from this position—every contraction, every spasm, every desperate flutter of muscles that have been pushed far beyond anything she's ever experienced before.

More fluid spurts from her pussy in hot, irregular bursts. It's not the controlled, sustained stream from before, but these sudden, violent pulses that seem to sync with her broken cries. Each one soaks me further, drenching my suit. The heat of it registers somewhere in the back of my mind, but I'm too focused on her—on the way her body is responding, the way she's completely lost to this—to care about the mess.

"That's it," I murmur, my voice rough and low, barely audible over her cries. "Let it happen. Don't fight it."

I'm going to replay this exact moment—her body arching, her pussy gushing, those broken sounds tearing from her throat—in my mind every single time I jerk off for the rest of my fucking life.

She surrenders completely, her voice breaking into a slow, low moan that reverberates through her entire frame. It's the sound of utter exhaustion, of a body and mind pushed past every conceivable limit. The moan deepens into something guttural, almost primal—spent, wrecked, emptied of everything she had left to give.

Then, without warning, the moaning fractures into something else entirely.

Crying. Long, wrenching sobs that shake her entire body. Tears stream down her flushed cheeks, cutting hot tracks through the sheen of sweat that covers her skin. Her face crumples, and the sounds coming from her throat are raw, unfiltered—the kind of crying that comes from somewhere deep and unguarded.

I withdraw my fingers slowly, carefully, feeling the aftershocks still rippling through her inner walls as I slide free. Moving around to the side of the exam table, I don't hesitate. I scoop her up in my arms, lifting her trembling, boneless form against my chest as though she weighs nothing. She curls into me immediately, instinctively, her small hands grasping desperately at my wet coat, fingers digging in like she's afraid I might let go.

I carry her over to the nearby couch—a low, leather piece positioned specifically for aftercare—and settle down with her cradled against me. Her body molds to mine, tucking perfectly into the curve of my chest and lap, her face pressed against my shoulder as she continues to sob.

"You're such a good girl," I murmur, my voice dropping low and soft, smoothing over her like a balm. I stroke her hair with deliberate, soothing motions, my fingers combing through the damp, tangled strands. "You came so beautifully. You gave me everything, didn't you? You got your wet heat all over me—covered me completely in your scent."

She cries harder at my words, her sobs intensifying, her shoulders shaking violently against me.

I shush her gently, leaning down to press a soft, lingering kiss to her forehead. The tenderness of the gesture surprises even me—it's not calculated, not part of the script I've been running in my head. It's just... instinct. A need to comfort her, to bring her back from wherever she's gone.

But my fucking god.

When a woman explodes all over you like that—drenches you in her hot heat, covers you so completely in her release that you can feel it soaking through every layer of fabric, feel it cooling on your skin—it does something to you. She responded to my finger and a pen.

Not even my cock.

I haven't even touched her with my cock yet, and this is what she gave me.

This is the kind of surrender she's capable of.

I continue petting her hair, smoothing it back from her tear-streaked face, my palm sliding down the damp length of it with slow, repetitive strokes. Her whole body is slick with sweat, and her own come, and tears, glistening in the low light, and I fucking love it.

I love the evidence of what just happened written all over her skin, love the way she smells—sex, and salt, and something uniquely her.

I love the way she's clinging to me now, like I'm the only solid thing in the world.

"You're mine," I whisper against her temple, my voice rough and low, stripped of its usual control. The words aren't a question. They're not a request. They're just truth—raw and absolute. "This just proves it. What you just did for me... what your body just gave me without me even asking..."

I press my lips to her hairline, breathing her in—sweat, and sex, and something darker, more primal. She's still trembling, little aftershocks running through her like electrical currents, and I can feel every single one of them where she's plastered against my chest.

"You couldn't fake that if you tried," I murmur, my hand still stroking, still soothing. "You couldn't hold that back. You're supposed to be mine for twenty-four hours, but your body just proved that this is forever. You belong to me already."

She goes still, finally. Completely spent. But then I feel it— the way she burrows her head deeper into my chest, turning her face away, pressing herself against me not in surrender but in retreat.

Hiding.

Oh. Oh, no. Absolutely fucking not. She does not get to hide from this. Not from what just happened. Not from what her body just proved.

"Look at me," I command, my voice cutting through the post-orgasmic haze with the sharp edge of authority.

She shakes her head against my chest, still breathing heavily, ragged and uneven. Refusing.

"Scarletta." I let her name roll off my tongue like a warning, dark and deliberate. "Either you look me in the eyes right now, or I will pry them open with an eye speculum. Don't make me do that, you beautiful little slut. I don't *want* to hurt you—not like that—but if you earn it, I'll be forced to balance the scales."

The words slip out without thought, unplanned and raw, pulled from somewhere deep and instinctive. The threat hangs between us, unexpected even to me.

A beat of silence. Then her eyes snap to mine—wide, shocked, darkened with lingering pleasure and something sharper. Her voice comes out low and gravelly, roughened by screaming. "Wh...*What*?"

Perfect. There she is.

I stroke her hair again, gentler now, and I smile beneath the ski mask, satisfaction radiating off me. "There she is. See? I knew you could follow directions." My voice drops into a purr, warm and approving. "That's a very good girl, Scarletta. You squirted your release all over me. I'm absolutely soaking wet."

"Oh, god," she moans, and I watch the embarrassment flood her face—cheeks flushing darker, eyes squeezing shut again as if she can erase what just happened by refusing to see it.

"Don't look away, Scarletta," I murmur, my tone warm with admiration even as my hand tightens possessively in her hair—not painful, just firm enough to keep her exactly where I want her. "This is a beautiful gift. Have you ever squirted before? I've never seen you do it, but perhaps you have. In the days before me, when you thought no one was watching."

The words slip out deliberately this time, calculated and precise. I watch their impact, the way understanding begins to dawn in those beautiful hazel eyes.

She's still looking at me, held captive by my grip and the weight of what I've just admitted. Then her eyes narrow down into dangerous little slits, confusion sharpening into comprehension and then fury.

"*What*?" The word comes out strangled, disbelieving. "What the hell are you talking about? You've *never seen me do it*? The times before you? What does that *mean*?"

She struggles in my grip, trying to push herself up and out of my lap, her body suddenly rigid with adrenaline-fueled panic. But I hold her absolutely still, my arm like iron across her waist, my hand firm and unyielding in her hair. My voice drops lower, darker, tolerating no disobedience. "Do not move."

She freezes—not from obedience, but from shock. Her breathing comes harder now, shallow and quick, her pupils dilating as fear crashes into the post-orgasmic haze still softening her edges.

"What does that mean?" she demands, her voice rising, cracking slightly. "The time before—have you been... *spying on me*?"

"Of course I have." The confession rolls off my tongue smooth and easy, like we're discussing the weather. "I put cameras in your apartment six months ago."

I watch the words hit her. Watch them process. Watch her face shift from confusion, to horror, to something sharper, more dangerous.

"I've read all your stories, ScarletSins." I let the username sit between us, deliberate and heavy. "I've watched you write them too. Fingering yourself during that scene in 'Bend Me Over'—you know the one, where Marcus bends Isla over the desk and fucks her while she's trying to finish her essay. You got so wet writing that scene you had to stop three times to make yourself come."

Her mouth opens, but no sound emerges. She's gone pale beneath the flush of exertion, her eyes wide and glassy.

I keep going, my voice dropping lower, more intimate. "The way you humped your pillow every day for a week when you wrote 'Two at a Time.' Every single day, Scarletta. Sometimes twice. You'd finish a chapter, post it, then read the comments while grinding against that sad little pillow like it could give you what you actually needed."

"Stop," she whispers, the word barely audible.

"Do you crave two at a time, Scarletta?" I tilt my head, considering her with clinical interest even as my cock throbs against the wet fabric of my boxers. "Two cocks filling you up, stretching you, using you? Is that what gets you off when you write those scenes? Imagining being so thoroughly fucked that you can't even think straight?"

She's shaking now—not from pleasure anymore, but from rage mixed with terror. Her hands push against my chest, weak and ineffectual. "Let me go."

"I'm afraid sharing is out of the question," I continue, ignoring her pathetic attempts to escape my grip. "But I'd be more than happy to stuff your ass with my cock while fucking your pussy with a dildo. Would that satisfy the fantasy? Would that be enough to scratch that particular itch you've been writing about for years?"

Something snaps in her.

She wrenches herself sideways with sudden, desperate strength—the kind that only comes from pure adrenaline and survival instinct. Her small body twists in my grip, slippery with sweat and her own release, and she manages to slip free. She hits the floor hard, stumbling, her legs still weak and unsteady from the orgasms I just wrung out of her.

But she doesn't fall.

She runs.

Laughter erupts from my chest before I can stop it—deep, and genuine, and utterly delighted. The sound fills the playroom, bouncing off the concrete walls and padded panels, echoing back at us in a way that probably sounds absolutely fucking unhinged.

I don't care.

This is perfect. This is exactly what I wanted without even knowing I wanted it.

"That's it!" I call after her, my voice ringing with dark amusement. "Run, little slut! Run!"

She pivots, her eyes wild and desperate, scanning the playroom for an exit. Her gaze lands on the sliding glass door at the far end first—the one that leads to the small outdoor patio area, currently buried under two feet of Wyoming snow.

She sprints toward it.

I don't chase her yet. I just stand there, watching, my chest heaving with laughter and exertion and something darker, more primal. My cock is rock-hard now, straining against my soaked slacks, and the sight of her naked body running from me—thighs still glistening with her own come, ass bouncing with each frantic step—is the most erotic thing I've ever witnessed.

She reaches the sliding door and grabs the handle, yanking hard.

It doesn't move.

She yanks again, harder this time, her whole body throwing itself into the effort. The door remains firmly locked, the mechanism controlled by a keypad she doesn't have the code for.

"No, no, no," she gasps, her voice rising in pitch. She pounds on the glass with her fists, as if that might somehow make it open. As if the freezing wilderness on the other side would be preferable to staying in here with me.

I start walking toward her. Not running. Not rushing. Just moving with slow, measured steps that eat up the distance between us with predatory inevitability.

She hears me coming.

Her head whips around, and when she sees me approaching—sees the deliberate, unhurried pace of my advance—pure terror floods her features. She abandons the door and darts sideways, running along the wall, putting the bondage table between us.

I adjust my trajectory, following her with the same methodical pace, as I slip my suit coat off and let it drop to the floor. I'm not trying to catch her yet. I'm herding her. Cornering her. Letting her tire herself out while I conserve my energy and enjoy the show.

"You're making this so much better than I imagined," I tell her conversationally, my voice carrying easily across the space between us as I pull my shirt out of my pants and unbutton it. "I knew you'd written chase scenes—'Hunted,' 'The Cottage,' that short piece called 'Prey'—but I wasn't sure if you'd actually enjoy being chased in real life."

She's panting now, her chest heaving, her eyes darting around the room looking for escape routes that don't exist. "You're insane," she spits out, her voice shaking. "You're a fucking psychopath."

"Probably," I agree easily, still advancing, letting the shirt slide down my arms. "But you already knew that, didn't you? You knew what you were signing up for when you clicked that confirmation button. When you filled out that questionnaire. When you got in the helicopter."

She moves again, circling around the St. Andrew's Cross, trying to keep furniture between us. Her legs are trembling— whether from exhaustion, fear, or the aftereffects of multiple orgasms, I'm not sure. Probably all three.

"I didn't sign up for this!" she shouts, her voice cracking. "I didn't consent to being stalked! To having cameras in my home! To—to—"

"To having your darkest fantasies brought to life?" I interrupt, my tone almost gentle. "To being hunted by someone who knows every sick, twisted thought you've ever had? To being cornered and claimed by a man who's read every word you've written about wanting exactly this?"

I shift direction, cutting her off before she can dart toward the suspension rig. She backpedals, stumbling slightly, and I watch her catch herself against the padded wall.

"You wrote seventeen different versions of this scene, Scarletta," I continue, still moving toward her with that same inexorable pace. "Seventeen different stories where the protagonist is chased, caught, claimed. Where she runs knowing she'll be caught. Where she fights knowing she'll lose. Where she surrenders knowing it's inevitable."

"Those are stories," she says, her back now pressed against the wall, her hands spread flat against the padding as if she could somehow push through it. "They're not real! They're fantasies!"

"Are they?" I stop walking, standing about ten feet away from her. Close enough that she can see every detail of my now exposed body—the tattoos covering my torso, the wet fabric of my slacks clinging to my erection, the predatory stillness in the way I'm watching her. "Because from where I'm standing, you look exactly like the heroines in your stories. Naked. Terrified. Aroused."

"I'm not aroused," she lies, but even from here I can see the evidence. Her nipples are hard peaks, her thighs pressed together, the telltale shine of wetness between her legs.

"Your body says differently." I take another step forward. "Your pussy is dripping, Scarletta. You're scared, yes. But you're also turned on. Just like Sally when Brett chased her through the woods. Just like Claire when her captor hunted her through the abandoned warehouse. Just like every single protagonist you've ever written who ran from a man who already owned her."

She shakes her head violently, her hair whipping around her face. "No. No, that's different. That's—"

"Different how?" Another step. "Because those women wanted it? Because they secretly hoped to be caught? Because they were running *toward* their fate instead of away from it?"

She opens her mouth, closes it, opens it again. No words come out.

"You're not different from them," I say softly, taking two more steps that bring me within arm's reach. "You're exactly the same. You're just too afraid to admit it."

She bolts.

Tries to, anyway. She ducks under my arm and makes a desperate sprint toward the open space near the cage, her feet sliding slightly on the smooth concrete. But she's exhausted now, her movements sloppy and uncoordinated, and I'm fresh, and patient, and have been planning this for six months.

I catch her easily.

My hand closes around her upper arm, spinning her around to face me. She immediately starts fighting—clawing at my chest, trying to knee me in the groin, her small fists pounding against my torso with surprising force.

I let her.

I stand there and take every hit, every scratch, every desperate attempt to hurt me. The pain barely registers. Her nails rake across my chest, probably leaving marks on the tattoos, and all I feel is satisfaction that she's finally showing me the real her—the one who fights back, who doesn't just submit quietly, who has fire underneath all that anxiety and self-doubt.

"That's it," I murmur, catching her wrists when she aims for my face. "Fight me. Show me what you've got."

"I hate you!" she screams, still struggling. "I hate you, I hate you, I—"

And that's when she notices the ink.

Her struggling falters. Her breathing changes. I feel the exact moment her brain registers what she's seeing—her palms pressed flat against my chest, her eyes going wide as they track across the images covering my torso.

Women bound. Women choked. Women on their knees

with cocks in their mouths. Women bent over furniture, hands cuffed behind their backs. Women displayed on St. Andrew's crosses, legs spread wide. Women with ball gags turning their screams into muffled whimpers. Women suspended from ceiling hooks, helpless and exposed.

All of them wearing the same face.

Her face.

The curve of her jaw. The slope of her neck. The exact shape of her lips. The way her eyes look when they're glazed with fear and arousal. Every piece of ink on my body is her—bound, used, claimed, worshipped through violence and control.

"What the..." Her voice is barely a whisper. She's not fighting anymore. Not even breathing properly. Just staring at the artwork covering my chest, my arms, my ribs. Her fingers trace one image involuntarily—a woman's throat caught in a man's grip, her back arched, her mouth open in what could be pleasure or pain. "What the hell is this?"

"You," I say simply.

Her eyes snap up to mine, wild and disbelieving. "But these—these are old. This ink is... some of this has to be years old."

I don't deny it. "Yes."

She's shaking her head now, trying to process. Her gaze drops back to my body, cataloging each piece. A woman on her knees, hands bound, looking up with submission written across her features. A woman bent over a bondage table, ass in the air, red marks blooming across her skin. A woman hanging from suspension cuffs, toes barely touching the ground.

All her. Every single one.

"You've had me tattooed on your body," she breathes, her voice cracking on the last word. "For years. Before you ever spoke to me. Before the auction. Before—"

"Before I even knew your real name," I confirm. "Before I

even knew your stories. Your fantasies. Your desires. It was you, in my dreams, for years. And now... you're here."

Her hands are trembling against my chest now, her fingers still tracing the images as if she can't quite believe they're real. "This is insane. This is—you're obsessed."

"Yes." I let the word hang in the cold air between us, let it sink into her bones like the ink has sunk into mine. I wait until her gaze drags up from the tattooed image of her own bound body to meet my eyes. When she does, I hold her there with nothing but the weight of my stare. "I'm obsessed. More than obsessed." I pause deliberately, letting each word land with the full force of its meaning. "I'm going to keep you."

Her breath catches. "Going to... going to keep me?" The question comes out strangled, disbelieving. "Like—like kidnap me?"

"Now, now," I murmur, my tone deceptively gentle, the kind of soothing voice you'd use to calm a frightened animal. "Let's not be dramatic. I don't need to kidnap you." I let my thumb brush slowly across her hipbone, feeling the way she shivers beneath the touch. "You came here of your own free will. Signed the contract. Walked into my home with your eyes wide open."

"I was literally blindfolded!" Her voice cracks, rises in pitch. "And I want to leave."

"You can leave," I say evenly, reasonably. My fingers still moving in those maddening, lazy circles against her skin. "When I'm done with you."

Her whole body goes rigid. "What if I want to leave right now?"

I tilt my head slightly, studying her with the kind of patience I've perfected over years of negotiations. "We've already been through this."

"I do!" The words explode out of her, sudden and fierce, and she tries to pull away from my touch. "I want to leave—"

Before the word can fully form on her lips, I've moved. My

hand slides from her hip to wrap around her waist, pulling her forward with enough force that she stumbles into me. In the same fluid motion, my other hand moves between her thighs, fingers finding her entrance and sliding up inside her in one smooth, deliberate thrust.

Two fingers curve upward immediately, pressing hard against that sensitive spot I've already memorized, dragging through the slick evidence of her arousal.

The effect is instantaneous. Her entire body seizes, that fierce defiance evaporating like steam. Her legs buckle, knees going weak, and she would collapse if I weren't holding her up.

Her fingers scramble for purchase against my tattooed chest, nails digging in as her body twists and writhes against the invasion. She's panting now, harsh desperate gasps as her pussy clenches rhythmically around my fingers, as her hips rock forward involuntarily seeking more contact even as her mind screams that she should be pulling away.

"There she is," I murmur against her ear, walking her backward step by step, my fingers never stopping their relentless motion inside her. "There's my good little slut."

She's coming apart completely now, helpless little whimpers spilling from her throat as I manipulate her body with practiced precision. When her back bumps against the white paper of the exam table she jerks in surprise, but I don't give her time to react. I just press her harder against it, my fingers curling deeper, my thumb finding her clit and circling with just enough pressure to make her cry out.

Her walls clench around me again, fluttering and grasping as another wave of pleasure crashes through her. She's soaking wet, my fingers sliding easily through her arousal, and the obscene sound of it fills the room.

When her trembling finally starts to subside, when she's nothing but a gasping, shaking mess supported entirely by my arm around her waist and my hand between her legs, I smile. Slow and satisfied.

"See?" I say softly, letting that smile bleed into my voice. "Such a good girl." I flex my fingers inside her once more, making her whimper. "We're right back where we started."

She barely manages to look over her shoulder at the exam table. Her head is heavy, her eyes are heavy, her feet probably feel like concrete.

I release her wrists and she doesn't run. Instead, her hands come up to grip my shoulders, her fingers digging in hard enough to bruise. Her whole body is trembling, caught between terror and desire, between what she thinks she should feel and what she actually feels.

I let her grab me. Let her hold her self up under my strength. "Tell me you want to leave," I command, my voice rough. "Tell me you want me to call the helicopter right now and send you home. Tell me you want nothing to do with this."

She stares at me, her mouth working soundlessly. Eyes barely able to focus.

"Say it," I press, one hand sliding down to grip her ass, pulling her harder against my erection. "Tell me to stop. Use your safeword. End this right now."

"I..." Her voice breaks as she gasps for breath. "I can't."

"Why not?"

"Because..." She squeezes her eyes shut, fresh tears spilling down her cheeks. "Because you're right. I'm such a fucking slut. You're right to call me that. I'm such a slut. I like this! I love it! I want you to do more! I do want this. I've always wanted this. But I'm terrified—"

"Of what?"

"Of you. Of myself. Of what it means that I'm turned on right now when I should be screaming for help. Of what kind of person that makes me."

I withdraw my fingers from her pussy and bring my hand

up to cup her face, my thumb brushing away her tears with surprising gentleness. "It makes you human, Scarletta. It makes you honest. It makes you exactly who you've always been in your stories—a woman brave enough to want what scares her."

"I'm not brave," she whispers. "I'm a coward. I hide from everything. I can't even pay my rent, or answer emails, or—"

"You got in the helicopter," I interrupt. "You signed the contract. You submitted yourself to the auction. You let me make you come so hard you squirted all over me. That's not cowardice. That's courage."

She laughs—a broken, desperate sound. "That's insanity."

"Maybe." I lean down, pressing my forehead against hers through the mask. "Or maybe it's the first honest thing you've done in years. Maybe this is the only place you can be real."

She's quiet for a long moment, her body still trembling against mine, her heart hammering so hard I can feel it against my chest.

"What happens now?" she finally asks, her voice small and uncertain.

I smile beneath the mask. "Now we finish your exam, little slut. But this time, I'm going to strap you down properly. Then I will make good on every promise I made. Of course, I'll have to punish you for running. Don't worry, my slut. I'll make sure you love it."

"But I get to go home, right?"

"Do you," I ask. Petting the side of her cheek. "Do you get to go home?"

Fear. Absolute fear. Her breath hitches. "I'm going to run again if you don't let me go home!"

"Then I'll chase you again." I slide my hand down her body, between her legs, feeling the slick evidence of her arousal. "And catch you again. And fuck you again. As many times as it takes until you understand that you're mine. That you've always been mine. That every word you've ever written was a letter addressed to me."

She whimpers—a sound of pure need that goes straight to my cock.

"But first," I murmur, my fingers circling her clit with deliberate pressure, "I want to hear you say it. I want to hear you admit what you are."

"What I am?" she gasps, her hips already moving against my hand.

"A good little slut who gets wet when she's chased. Who comes harder when she's scared. Who needs to be owned by someone who knows all her secrets." I increase the pressure, watching her face carefully. "Say it."

"I... I can't..."

"Yes, you can." I pinch her clit—not hard enough to hurt, but enough to make her gasp. "Say it, or I stop touching you right now and chain you to a wall until you're ready to be honest."

Her eyes fly open, meeting mine with desperate intensity.

"Do you doubt me, Scarletta?" I ask, my voice dropping to something cold and dangerous. "Have I proven myself to be a capable Master?" I let the silence stretch between us, watching the way her pupils dilate with something between fear and arousal. "Or am I just another Derek?"

The name of her ex strikes her like a physical blow. I watch the fear bloom in her eyes—real fear, not the delicious kind that makes her wet. She'd forgotten about him in the haze of endorphins and adrenaline.

Now she remembers.

Now she understands the difference.

Her breath catches, and then she starts to cry—not the pretty tears from before, but the ugly, gasping kind that come from somewhere deep and wounded. "Why are you doing this to me?"

I lean in and kiss her mouth, tasting salt and surrender.

She tastes like her own come, and sweat, and desperation—and I fucking love it. "Because you like it, Scarletta," I murmur against her lips. "Because you need it. Because every fantasy you've ever written was begging for someone to make you live it." I pull back just enough to look into her eyes. "Now say it."

"I don't—" she starts, but I cut off her protest with deliberate action.

I finger her harder, pumping up, curling my fingertips against that spot that makes her entire body arch. She nearly falls over from the intensity—her legs trembling, her breath coming in sharp gasps. She's so over-sensitized from the chase, from coming and squirting, from the terror and the surrender. It's phenomenal. Every nerve ending is alive, every touch amplified beyond bearing.

"I'm..." She swallows hard, fighting against her own shame even as her body clenches around my fingers. "I'm a good little slut who gets wet when she's chased."

"And?" I prompt, my thumb finding her clit and circling with exactly the right pressure to make her gasp.

"And I come harder when I'm scared," she admits, her voice breaking on the words.

"And?" I slow my movements, making her chase the friction, making her work for it.

"And I need..." Her voice drops to barely a whisper, as if saying it quietly will make it less true. "I need to be owned by someone who knows all my secrets."

"Good girl." I reward her with two fingers sliding inside her pussy, curling up to hit that spot that makes her knees buckle. "Such a good, honest girl. Now let's get you properly restrained so I can really make you scream."

CHAPTER 15
SCARLETTA

There's something fundamentally, irreversibly wrong with me. I don't even try to fight—not a single token protest, not even the pretense of resistance—when he presses his large, strong hands into my hips, fingers digging into the soft flesh there, and lifts me up onto the exam table as though I weigh nothing at all.

The white sanitary paper crinkles loudly under my ass and the backs of my thighs, the sound obscenely innocent in this room designed for depravity, but there's no time to think about that trivial detail, because master is already pushing me backwards with inexorable force, his hand flat against the small of my back, supposedly guiding me down onto the padded leather surface.

It's a stupid gesture that means absolutely nothing, a mockery of tenderness, because he's not being gentle.

He's a monster in a mask.

Then, just when I think I've experienced the depths of degradation, the humiliation starts all over again, fresh and cutting.

He straightens my legs with clinical efficiency, running his palms down the length of them from hip to ankle, then deliberately pries my knees apart, spreading them wide. His movements are unhurried, methodical. He gently cups each heel in turn—such a careful, almost reverent touch that makes this somehow worse—and places them precisely in the waiting stirrups, positioning me exactly as he wants me.

I close my eyes. Tight. Squeezing them shut hard enough that colors burst behind my eyelids.

"Look at me, little slut. Eyes up." His voice cuts through my attempt at mental escape.

I open them, surrendering even this small rebellion. I'm so fucking tired of fighting, exhausted down to my bones. If he wants to spread my pussy open with a speculum and examine me like I'm a specimen, maybe I should just let him and get it over with.

The bitter truth I'm learning is that the more I fight, the more he clearly likes it, the longer this entire ordeal will take.

Compliance might be my only path to mercy.

"You're going to watch in the mirror," he says. It's a command, simple and absolute.

So I do exactly what I'm told. I watch, because I have no choice, as he straps my ankles to the stirrups with practiced efficiency. First one ankle, leather tightening with a soft creak, then the other, the symmetry of my captivity somehow making it worse. Then he moves with predatory grace up towards my head, his fingers circle my wrist—warm, firm, inescapable—bringing my arm clear above my head in a smooth arc, securing my wrist inside a heavy cuff that must be bolted directly to the wall or the table's frame, because it doesn't shift even a fraction when I instinctively test it.

He does the same for the other one, completing my bondage with the same unhurried certainty.

And there it is, reflected back at me in merciless detail.

Me.

Spread eagle. Utterly helpless. Completely exposed.

Every vulnerable inch of me on display.

"What happens next?" Master asks, his voice cutting through the haze of my panic like a blade.

I blink up at him, my brain struggling to process the question. "What?"

"In your story, Scarletta." He shifts his weight, and I feel rather than see him studying me with that unnerving intensity. "Not the one you already wrote. The one you're writing right now. In your head. What happens next?"

My mind stutters, trying to catch up. He wants me to... write a story? A new story? Right now? Something just for him?

Well. This, at least, is something I'm good at. Even strapped down and terrified, my writer's brain can still function. "She—"

"Scarletta." His correction is sharp, immediate. "'She' is you. Call her by her name."

What a psycho. But I swallow hard and try again. "Scarletta is..." I breathe, my voice shakier than I want it to be. "She's strapped to an exam table and—"

"Be very careful what you say next." And do I catch the hint of a smirk playing at the edges of that mask? I think I do. The faintest curve of cruel amusement. "Because all stories come true tonight. Everything you say, I'll make happen. So if I were you, Scarletta... I'd dig deep into that filthy, brilliant brain of yours and come up with something you might never have the courage to ask for again."

I scoff. I mean, his self-confidence is almost obscene.

But he's not wrong. He's giving me permission—no, he's *demanding* that I confess what I want. What I've written a thousand times but never dared to experience. But my mind is scattered, thoughts fragmenting like dropped glass. "I... I can't think straight."

"Sure you can, little slut." His hand comes down to my brow, and the gentleness of the touch is almost worse than any cruelty. His fingers smooth some stray hair away from my eyes with surprising tenderness, the contrast making my breath catch. "You want to be fucked by me today, don't you?"

The question hangs in the air between us. Direct. Undeniable.

I exhale slowly, a shaky surrender of breath. *Just admit it, Scar. Just say it.* "Yes."

He smiles. This time, for sure, I know he smiles—I can see the way his eyes crinkle slightly at the corners, visible even through the mask. "Good girl. Now... how do you want me to start?"

I bite my lip, thinking, my mind racing through a thousand possibilities. Then I force myself to look him directly in the eyes, gathering what little courage I have left. "Let me see it first."

He actually laughs—a genuine sound of surprised pleasure that makes something flip in my stomach. But without a moment's hesitation, he reaches down and pulls his cock out of his pants, fisting it confidently in his hand. He moves closer, bringing it near enough that I could touch it if my hands weren't bound, close enough that I can see every detail.

"It's nice, don't you think?" he asks, his voice dropping to something darker, rougher.

I stare at the absolute monster of a thing in his hand, my eyes widening despite myself. My fucking god. He's *massive*. Thick, and long, and already hard, the head flushed dark with arousal. The kind of cock I've written about but never actually encountered in real life. The kind that makes me simultaneously terrified and desperately, shamefully curious.

"Where should I put it first?" he whispers, and the question alone makes my breath catch in my throat.

Before I can formulate an answer—before I can even process what he's asking—he moves forward. "Here?"

The thick, hot length of him touches my lips, and I gasp at the contact. My mouth opens instinctively, automatically, like my body is responding to commands my brain hasn't even registered yet. But he doesn't push inside, doesn't take advantage of my parted lips.

Instead, he traces them slowly with just the tip. Deliberate. Teasing. I can feel how slick he is, pre-cum smearing across my bottom lip in a wet trail that makes me shudder. The sensation is filthy, and intimate, and overwhelming. And when a drop slides off my lip and trails down over the curve of my chin, I make a small, helpless sound in the back of my throat.

"Here?" he asks again, and this time his cock drags across my skin as he moves it downward. The heat of him brands a path down my throat, over my collarbone, until he's touching the stiff peak of my nipple with the same teasing, circular motion. The contrast between the soft, velvety head and my sensitive flesh makes me arch against the restraints, trying to get more contact even as I know I shouldn't.

"Or here?" His voice has dropped even lower now, rough with arousal as he walks around to position himself between my spread knees. I watch in the mirror, feeling *everything* at the same time. The brush of his thighs against the inside of my legs. The way he dips down, bringing his cock to my clit and circling it with the same maddening, barely-there pressure he used on my lips.

The sensation rips a whimper from my throat. I'm so wet already that he glides easily against me, the thick head of him pressing and retreating, pressing and retreating, until I'm trembling and biting the inside of my cheek so hard, I taste copper.

"There are a few more ways to play this one out, if you're adventurous enough," he continues conversationally, like he isn't driving me absolutely insane with need. Like he can't hear the desperate little sounds I'm making or feel how my hips are trying to tilt toward him despite the restraints holding me in place.

"Would you like me to go on? Should I show you all your options before you decide? Or have you already made up your mind about where you want this cock first, my sweet little slut?"

I force myself to speak, my voice coming out small and broken. "What... what are my other options?"

His answering smile is pure wickedness, visible in the slight tilt of his head, the way his eyes gleam behind that fucking mask.

"I'm so glad you asked." His voice is low, rough with arousal. "Because I have *so* many ideas for this perfect little body of yours."

I watch in the mirror as he takes his cock in hand, stroking it slowly while he studies me. Then he moves lower, and oh god, oh fuck, I feel the thick head of him press against my asshole.

Just the tip. Just enough pressure to make me gasp and tense against the restraints.

"I could fuck this tight little hole instead," he says conversationally, like he's discussing the weather. "Stretch you open slowly. Make you feel every single inch as I work my way inside. You've written about it, haven't you? How it hurts at first, that burning stretch that makes you cry? But then how it starts to feel good in that dark, shameful way you crave?"

He pushes slightly harder, just enough that I feel my body start to give way, and I make a desperate sound that's half whimper, half plea.

"I'd go slow at first," he continues, his voice dropping even lower. "Let you adjust. Let you feel how full you are, how completely I'm claiming every hole. Then I'd fuck you properly—hard and deep until you're sobbing, and begging, and you don't even know if you want me to stop or keep going."

My breath is coming in short, sharp gasps. The pressure is constant, insistent, not quite pushing inside but making it very clear that he could. That all it would take is one firm thrust and he'd be buried in my ass whether I was ready or not.

"Or," he says, pulling away suddenly, leaving me gasping at the loss of contact. He moves up toward my head, and I crane my neck to watch as he brings his cock to my mouth again. "I could fuck your throat instead."

The tip touches my lips, and I can taste myself on him—salt and musk and something darker.

"Not your mouth, Scarletta. Your *throat*." He emphasizes the word, making sure I understand the distinction. "I'd grip your hair like this—" His free hand tangles in my hair, pulling my head back at an angle that makes my neck straighten. "And I'd slide in deep. Past your tongue, past your gag reflex. I'd hold myself there while you choke, and your eyes water, and you can't breathe around my cock."

My heart is hammering against my ribs. I can barely process what he's saying.

"You'd drool everywhere," he continues, almost dreamily. "Spit would be running down your chin, tears streaming down your pretty face. And I'd fuck your throat like it's a pussy—hard and brutal until you're gagging and struggling and making those desperate little sounds. Then I'd come down your throat and make you swallow every drop."

I'm shaking now, trembling so hard the restraints rattle slightly.

"Of course," he says, releasing my hair and stepping back, "if you really want to commit to this experience..." He walks over to a cabinet I hadn't noticed before and opens it, revealing an array of toys that makes my stomach drop. "I have options."

He pulls out a thick purple dildo, holding it up so I can see it clearly in the mirror. It's huge—maybe not quite as big as his cock, but close enough to make me whimper.

"I could strap this one to myself," he explains, walking

back to position himself between my legs. "Fuck your pussy with my cock while this one stretches your ass. Both holes at once, Scarletta. Completely filled. Two at a Time, remember?"

He sets that dildo aside and picks up another one—this one slimmer but longer, with a flared base.

"Or I could put this one in your ass, fuck your pussy myself, and stick a dildo down your throat at the same time." His voice has taken on a darker edge now, getting rougher as his arousal builds. "All three holes filled. Unable to move, unable to speak, unable to do anything but take it. Just like you wrote in 'Debased.' Remember that one? Where the protagonist is strapped down and used by three men at once?"

I do remember. Of course I fucking remember. I wrote it two months ago during one of my darkest spirals, posting it at 3 AM and immediately regretting it.

"I'd make you watch yourself in the mirror," he continues relentlessly. "Watch as you're completely used. Watch your body betray you, getting wetter and wetter even as you're overwhelmed and crying. Watch yourself come so hard you black out."

My mind is spinning, fractured images overlapping—his cock in my ass, dildos filling me everywhere, my own words weaponized against me.

"Or," he says, setting the toys aside and running his hand along the inside of my thigh, "we could start simpler. Just this —" His fingers trace my dripping pussy lips, making me gasp. "Just my cock in your pussy. Nice and traditional for your first time with me. Let you get used to how I feel before we graduate to the truly filthy shit you've been writing about."

He leans over me, bringing his face close to mine, his masked features filling my vision.

"So what will it be, little slut? Where do you want this cock first?"

I'm trembling, my mind racing through all the options he's laid out. Each one more terrifying and arousing than the last. Each one pulled directly from my own twisted fantasies.

But I know what I want. What I can handle. What won't completely destroy me in the first hour of this twenty-four hour contract.

"Just..." My voice cracks. I swallow hard and try again. "Just vaginal. Just your cock in my pussy. Please."

"Please what?" he prompts, his hand still stroking my inner thigh.

I close my eyes, feeling the heat of shame flood my face. "Please fuck my pussy, Master."

"Good girl," he murmurs, and I hear the smile in his voice. "Such a good, honest little slut. Choosing what you actually want instead of trying to impress me. I appreciate that."

He positions himself between my legs again, and I feel the thick head of his cock press against my entrance. Not pushing in yet, just resting there, making me feel how big he is, how completely he's going to fill me.

"But Scarletta?" His voice drops to something darker, something that makes my breath catch. "This is just the beginning. Before this night is over, I'm going to fuck every hole you have. I'm going to use every toy in that cabinet. I'm going to make you beg for things you're too scared to choose right now."

The tip of him pushes inside, just barely, and I gasp at the stretch.

"But for now," he says softly, "I'm going to fuck this pretty little pussy until you scream."

And then he does.

The thick head of his cock pushes inside me, and I feel myself stretch around him—too much, god, too much—but he doesn't stop. He just keeps pushing, slow and relentless, until I'm making these desperate little sounds I don't recognize.

"Breathe," he commands, his hand sliding up to my throat. Not squeezing, just resting there. A reminder. "You can take it."

I can't. I fucking can't. He's too big, too much, and I'm going to split apart—

But then he's fully inside me, buried to the hilt, and I can feel every fucking inch of him. My pussy clenches around him involuntarily, and he groans—the first sound of his own pleasure I've heard all night.

"Good girl," he murmurs, staying completely still. Letting me adjust. Letting me feel how completely he's filling me. "Such a good little slut, taking all of me."

Then he starts to move.

Slow at first. Long, deep strokes that make me gasp with each thrust. I watch in the mirror, mesmerized and horrified by the sight of his cock sliding in and out of me, glistening with my wetness.

His fingers find my clit.

The touch is electric, overwhelming, and I cry out—an actual scream that echoes off the walls. He circles my clit with the same deliberate precision he's using to fuck me, matching the rhythm of his hips with the movement of his fingers.

"That's it," he says, his voice rougher now. "Let me hear you."

The pleasure builds fast—too fast. That weird feeling of pure bliss starting somewhere deep in my core and spreading outward like wildfire. His cock pumps harder now, faster, hitting something inside me that makes my vision blur.

Then his other hand is on my breast, twisting my nipple hard enough to make me gasp. The sharp pain mingles with the overwhelming pleasure, creating something dark and twisted that I don't have words for.

His fingers slide up from my throat to my mouth, pushing past my lips. I taste myself on them—salt and musk and something darker—and I suck instinctively, my tongue swirling around his fingers even as his cock pounds into me relentlessly.

He's everywhere at once. Filling my pussy, stimulating my clit, twisting my nipple, fingers in my mouth, pushing deeper until I gag slightly. Every nerve ending in my body is firing at the same time, and I can't—I can't—

"Come for me," he commands, his voice dark and absolute. "Come on my cock like a good little slut."

And I do.

The orgasm crashes over me with the force of a tidal wave, and I see white. Literally white. My vision goes completely blank, my body convulsing so hard the restraints bite into my ankles and wrists. I'm screaming around his fingers in my mouth, or maybe I'm not making any sound at all—I can't tell anymore, can't distinguish between what's real and what's sensation.

Everything goes black.

I wake up gasping for air.

He's still fucking me.

Still buried deep inside me, his cock moving in and out with the same relentless rhythm, his fingers still working my clit. How long was I out? Seconds? Minutes? I can't tell, can't think, can't—

"There she is," he says, and I can hear the smile in his voice. "Welcome back."

The pleasure hasn't stopped. It never stopped. My body is still riding the wave of that orgasm, or maybe it's a new one building—I can't distinguish anymore where one ends and another begins.

"I told you I'd fuck you until you scream," he continues conversationally, like he isn't destroying me. "You passed out. Did you know that? Your whole body just went limp. It was beautiful."

His fingers press harder on my clit, and I feel it building

again—that impossible, overwhelming sensation that my body can't possibly sustain.

"Let's see if we can make it happen again," he murmurs.

And then he's twisting my nipple hard, grinding his cock deep inside me, rubbing my clit in fast, brutal circles—

I come again.

See white.

Everything dissolves.

When I surface this time, there's something pressed against my lips.

A sippy straw.

I blink hazily, trying to focus. He's holding a cup of water, his cock still buried inside me but not moving now. Just there. Keeping me full while I drink.

"Good girl," he coos softly, his voice gentle in a way that makes something crack in my chest. "Drink for me. You need to stay hydrated."

I drink obediently, the cool water soothing my raw throat. I didn't even realize how thirsty I was, how much I've been screaming and gasping and—

He pulls the cup away and sets it aside.

"Better?" he asks, brushing some sweat-dampened hair off my forehead with surprising tenderness.

I nod weakly, unable to form words.

"Good," he says. "Because we're not done yet."

And then he's fucking me again.

Harder this time. Faster. His hips slamming into me with bruising force, the sound of skin slapping against skin echoing obscenely in the room. I'm still sensitive from the last orgasms—too sensitive—and every thrust feels like too much and not enough at the same time.

"You're doing so well," he tells me, his voice rough with arousal. "Taking my cock so perfectly. Making such pretty sounds for me."

I am making sounds—desperate, broken little whimpers

and gasps that I have no control over. My body is acting on pure instinct now, my hips trying to meet his thrusts despite the restraints holding me in place.

The pleasure builds again, impossibly fast, and I try to speak, try to tell him it's too much, I can't—

But his fingers are back on my clit, and I'm lost.

I hear a sound.

A mechanical buzz that cuts through the fog in my brain.

I force my eyes open and see him holding something—a wand vibrator. Industrial-looking. The kind that plugs into the wall. The kind that looks relentless and unforgiving.

I gasp. "I can't—"

"You can," he says firmly. "And you will."

He presses the vibrator against my clit while his cock continues to pound into me, and the sensation is immediate and overwhelming and absolutely fucking unbearable.

I come instantly.

No build-up, no warning. Just a sudden, violent orgasm that rips through my body like lightning. I'm screaming, thrashing against the restraints, my pussy clenching around his cock so hard it almost hurts.

But he doesn't stop.

The vibrator stays pressed against my clit, relentless and unforgiving, and another orgasm crashes over me before the first one even finishes. Then another. Then another.

I can't stop coming.

Can't catch my breath, can't think, can't do anything but feel as wave after wave of pleasure-pain tears through my body. My vision is flickering—white, black, white, black—and I can hear myself making sounds I didn't know I was capable of.

"That's it," he groans, his voice strained now with his own approaching release. "Come for me. Keep coming. Don't fucking stop."

I couldn't stop if I wanted to.

The vibrator is merciless, the angle perfect, his cock hitting that spot deep inside me with every brutal thrust. I'm drowning in sensation, drowning in pleasure, drowning in him.

Another orgasm. Stronger than the last.

My body arches off the table as much as the restraints allow, every muscle locked tight, and I see pure white—

Everything goes black.

I wake up in someone's lap.

Warm. Solid. Moving.

His chest is rising and falling hard, like he just ran a marathon. Or came.

Oh god.

My body feels like rubber. Limp and useless. There's this weird buzzing sensation everywhere—aftershocks. Leftover orgasms still pulsing through my system like electrical currents that won't stop firing.

I try to move and can't. My muscles won't cooperate. Everything feels disconnected, like I'm operating a body I don't quite remember how to control.

How did I get here?

The last thing I remember is—

The vibrator. His cock. Coming so hard I saw white.

And then... nothing.

Just black.

How long was I out?

I blink, trying to focus. His hand is stroking my hair. Gentle. Possessive. Like I'm some kind of pet he's calming down after—

After what?

My mind starts working again, piecing together fragments. The exam table. The restraints. Him fucking me until I passed out.

And then nothing.

Nothing.

Oh god.

The realization hits me.

He drugged me.

He fucking *drugged* me.

That's the only explanation. You don't just black out like that. You don't lose hours—because it has to have been hours, my body feels wrecked in ways that couldn't have happened in minutes—you don't lose *time* unless something was done to you.

He fucked me while I was unconscious.

While I was *passed out.*

The panic slams into me all at once. Fight or flight. Every nerve ending that was buzzing with pleasure two seconds ago is now screaming *danger danger danger run run RUN.*

I move.

My body shouldn't be capable of it, but adrenaline is a hell of a thing. I'm suddenly up, stumbling off his lap, my legs barely supporting my weight but I'm *moving.*

"Scarletta—"

I don't look back.

The stairs. I see them now—completely open, leading up to the main floor. How did I miss them before? Doesn't matter. I'm running, my feet slapping against the wood, my thighs screaming in protest.

"Scarletta, wait—"

He's behind me. Following. I hear his footsteps, heavy and fast.

I reach the top of the stairs and keep going. The main floor is dark except for—

Windows.

I see light through the windows.

Natural light.

Morning.

It's fucking *morning.*

How many hours did I lose? The auction was mid morning. It should still be afternoon! It should be—

Oh god. Oh god oh god oh god.

I run harder, my vision tunneling on the front door. Just get to the door. Get outside. Flag down a car. Scream for help. Something. Anything.

"SCARLETTA, STOP!"

His voice is loud now, commanding, the same tone he used to make me come—

I scream.

Not words. Just pure sound. Terror ripping out of my throat as I hit the front door and yank it open.

Cold air slams into me like a physical force.

Snow. Everywhere. Blinding white in the early morning light.

I don't care.

I run.

My bare feet hit the snow and I can't feel them. Can't feel anything except the burning cold against my naked skin and the desperate need to get *away*.

He's calling my name. Still following.

I scream louder. "HELP! SOMEONE HELP ME!"

There's no one. Just mountains and trees and endless fucking snow.

I keep running anyway. My legs are giving out, muscles turned to jelly, but the adrenaline won't let me stop. I'm sobbing now, gasping for air that burns my lungs, my whole body on fire from the cold.

"SCARLETTA!"

He's closer.

Too close.

I try to run faster but my foot catches on something—a root, a rock, I don't know—and I stumble.

Then he's on me.

His weight slams into me from behind and we go down

hard, crashing into the snow. The impact knocks the air from my lungs and I can't breathe, can't scream, can't—

"No no no NO!" I'm kicking, thrashing, trying to get away. "GET OFF ME! HELP! SOMEONE—"

Something sharp pierces my thigh.

A pinch. A sting.

I see it in my peripheral vision—a syringe. He's pushing the plunger down, injecting something into my muscle.

"No," I gasp, still fighting. "No no no—"

The world starts to blur.

Edges going soft and fuzzy.

His face above me, the ski mask still on, his eyes visible now in the morning light. Blue. So fucking blue it doesn't make sense.

"I'm sorry," he's saying, but his voice sounds distant. Underwater. "I'm sorry, I didn't—you weren't supposed to—"

The words don't make sense.

Nothing makes sense.

My limbs are going heavy. Too heavy to fight anymore.

"Please," I whisper, but I don't know what I'm asking for.

The cold is disappearing. The fear is disappearing.

Everything is disappearing.

His face. The snow. The light.

All of it fading to black.

CHAPTER 16
SCARLETTA

I'm six years old and Daddy is building me a kingdom made of cotton flannel, and polyester blend, and rayon puffer sleeping bags—the softest materials in the whole house, all gathered up and draped like royal tapestries.

The walls of the kingdom are chair backs standing sentinel, cushions stacked like fortress stones, and broom handles propped at careful angles to hold everything together.

There's a moat—because every princess castle has a moat to keep the Dereks away.

The blanket fort stretches across the entire living room, swallowing up the coffee table and the ottoman and half the couch. The fabric glows amber from the flashlight he tucked inside somewhere, the beam diffused through layers of sheets and quilts, turning everything soft, and golden, and safe.

It's the most beautiful thing I've ever seen.

"This one goes here, Lettie-bug," he says, his voice distant and warm. His hands are huge, pinning the corner of Mom's good bedsheet to the bookshelf with a stack of encyclopedias.

I'm holding the other corner, standing on tiptoes, trying to reach.

Everything moves slow. Like underwater.

The sheet ripples and sways even though there's no breeze. Dad's face blurs at the edges when I try to look at him directly. But I know he's smiling. I can feel it.

"Will it be strong enough?" My voice sounds small. Far away.

"Strong enough for what, baby girl?"

"To keep the monsters out."

He laughs. The sound echoes and multiplies, bouncing around the dream-memory until there are a hundred versions of his laugh surrounding me.

"Ain't no monsters getting through this fort," he promises, crawling inside on his hands and knees. "Come on. Let me show you."

I follow him in.

The space inside is bigger than it should be. Impossibly big. The sheets stretch up and up like a cathedral ceiling, and the flashlight beam doesn't have a source anymore—it's just everywhere, golden and safe.

Daddy pulls me into his lap. He smells like coffee and Old Spice. "See?" He wraps his arms around me. "Nothing can hurt you in here. This is yours. Your space. Your world."

I lean back against his chest. His heartbeat is slow. Thump... thump... thump...

But it's not true.

Things can hurt you everywhere.

The world is filled with Dereks who slither under the water looking for cracks in your cushion foundation.

I'm going to tell my dad this. As a grown up now, not as a child, but when I look over my shoulder, he's gone.

I'm alone.

Like always.

And the moment this thought hits, the blankets start dissolving. Becoming transparent.

Wake up.

The thought cuts through the dream like a blade.

Wake up, wake up, WAKE UP—

The world comes back in pieces.

Sound first. A faint humming that feels familiar but I can't place it.

Then weight. My body pressed into something soft. A bed. My bed. I feel like I was in a car accident. My whole body is *sore.*

I want to look around and see where I am, but my eyes won't open. Way too heavy and crusted with bits of sleep that act like glue.

Move. Come on. Move.

The voice in my head sounds panicky. Like something is happening in the present—

Oh, shit!

Oh, shit, oh shit, oh shit!

Something *is* happening in the present—I'm being drugged!

I force my eyes to open—the crusty bits pulling on the sensitive skin of my lashes until finally, the tension breaks and… *light.* Too much light.

I turn my head away, blinking against the brightness, and wait for my vision to clear. A ceiling. Specifically, my ceiling. I'd recognize it anywhere. Ugly popcorn. Cobwebs. That little water stain in the corner that looks like an eyeball.

I'm home.

What—

I push myself up on my elbows. My head swims, vision tilting sideways before it corrects itself. My mouth is dry. My body feels... wrong. Like I've been asleep for days.

How did I get here?

I look down at myself.

Clothes, not naked. The sage green ribbed leggings I love to death, but haven't seen in months because they got swallowed by a dirty laundry pile. The soft sweatshirt—my favorite. The one with the embroidered flowers on the front that's been in the corner of my bathroom because I was too lazy to pick it up and wash it.

I'm wearing them.

But they're clean.

I didn't do laundry. I haven't done laundry in—

Something glitters in my peripheral vision.

I turn my head too fast. The room spins again.

There's a Christmas tree.

A small one on the little table in front of the window that used to have seven dead potted plants on it the last time I was here. It's about three feet tall. Real pine. The scent is… amazing.

It's decorated. Handmade felt ornaments hang from every branch. It's a garden theme. This year's theme. I do a Pinterest board every year called "Perfect Christmas Vibes" and fill it with the most dreamy Christmas decorations I can find on Etsy.

This year's theme is Spring Garden Christmas.

I know these ornaments.

The little brown mole with an armful of pink and yellow tulips clutched in his tiny felt paws. The Rabbit family wearing pastel waistcoats in mint green and lavender, each one clutching hand-stitched carrots with delicate embroidered tops.

A cheerful yellow rain boot overflowing with more tulips, their petals individually cut and layered.

There's a beekeeper in a tiny white suit with a miniature honey jar, and a garden Santa with a watering can instead of a sack, and a flower angel with wings made of layered petals and a daisy halo.

And felt ball flower garlands in soft pinks, creams, and yellows drape around the edges of the tree like a dreamy, whimsical daisy chain.

Each ornament is impossibly detailed. Hand-stitched.

They're also impossibly expensive. Handmade by a shop in Vermont called SuzieStiches.

I know this because I've been looking at these ornaments since July. Sometime around mid-summer, when the heat made everything feel unbearable and I needed to escape into something soft and magical, I started my annual Christmas Pinterest board. Every couple of weeks since then, I'd find myself scrolling through SuzieStiches' shop at two in the morning, adding these exact ornaments to my cart one by one. The mole. The rabbit family. The rain boot. The beekeeper. All of them.

Then I'd stare at the total—sometimes seven hundred dollars, sometimes nine hundred if I really went wild—and feel my stomach twist with something between longing and shame.

I'd leave them sitting in my cart for days, reopening the tab just to look at them, imagining how they'd look on a real tree in a real home where someone like me actually belonged.

Then I'd delete them. Every time.

I've lived the past four Christmases vicariously through my Pinterest board, curating perfect holidays I'll never have, saving images of homes that will never be mine.

But here they are.

Every single one of them.

On a tree.

A real tree, with real pine scent filling my apartment.

My apartment.

This isn't real. This isn't—

I swing my legs off the bed, then look back at it.

I was sleeping in it.

For a minute, I'm grossed out because those sheets have not been changed since... I can't even admit that in my own private thoughts.

Too long, let's just say.

But they're not the same sheets. They're flannel, and yellow, and I don't own yellow flannel sheets.

I stand. Too fast. My knees buckle and I catch myself on the edge of the mattress, breathing hard.

That's when I notice something else.

My apartment is *clean*.

Not clean like I picked up a little. Clean like someone came in and sorted through every single thing I own.

My books are stacked neatly on the shelf instead of scattered across the floor. The empty ramen cups are gone. The pile of laundry that's been sitting in the corner for three weeks—gone. It even smells good.

My apartment hasn't been clean since… well… ever.

It's just… not a priority when you're depressed.

This is when I notice my blanket fort is gone.

Gone, as in… been replaced.

It's a glamping tent now.

An actual miniature glamping tent. The kind you'd buy for a kid. Canvas walls printed with moons and stars. A peaked roof. An arched doorway with a rolled-back flap. Fairy lights string across the top, glowing soft white.

I take a step toward it. Then another.

My hand touches the fabric. It's real.

I crouch down and look inside.

The space is bigger than it should be. A child-sized tent but with room to sit up, move around. The floor is covered with a plush rug—white, furry, soft and thick enough to sink into.

In the center sits a wooden crate. Small. Perfectly sized to be a table.

My laptop is open on top of it.

The screen glows.

I crawl inside. The fairy lights cast everything in gentle shadows. It feels safe. Warm.

This is wrong.

I kneel in front of the laptop. The document is still open. The same scene I was writing before—

Before.

Before what?

My hands start shaking.

Think. Think.

The eviction notice. The auction. The helicopter.

The man in the mask.

The exam table.

His cock inside me. His fingers. The wand vibrator. Coming so hard I—

I blacked out.

And then I woke up and ran.

He chased me through the snow.

The syringe.

He drugged me.

I press my hands against my face. My skin is warm. Real.

He drugged me and brought me back here.

I crawl back out of the tent, stumbling to my feet.

My phone. Where's my phone?

I scan the room, pulse hammering.

There. On the kitchen counter.

I lunge for it, grab it, press the home button.

Unlocked. Fully charged.

The date stares back at me.

December 25th. 12:04 PM.

I sink onto the edge of a dining room chair that's actually by the table where it should be, instead of supporting my blanket fort.

He drugged me.

That's when I see what else is on the counter.

A plate of cookies.

Sugar cookies. The kind shaped like snowmen and Christmas trees. Frosted. White icing with red and green sprinkles.

One has a bite missing. A perfect half-moon carved out of the snowman's head.

Santa was here.

The thought lands before I can stop it. Childish. Stupid.

But I'm six years old again. Standing in my pajamas in the kitchen doorway, staring at the plate Daddy and I put out the night before with a glass of milk.

"See, Lettie-bug?" Daddy's voice, warm and conspiratorial. "Look!" He holds up the cookie with a bite taken out. Points to the glass of milk, half empty. "Told you he'd come."

I believed him. God, I believed him so hard.

My chest tightens.

I'm crying.

Why the fuck am I crying?

I press my palms against my eyes. Force myself to breathe. He's been dead for fourteen years, Scarletta. Fourteen fucking years. *Get a goddamned grip!*

I need to get over this. I need to—

Stop.

I drop my hands. Wipe my face with the back of my wrist.

There's a present next to the plate.

Small. Wrapped in matte black paper with a silver ribbon.

Ring-sized.

My stomach flips.

No. No way.

I pick it up with shaking hands.

My mind is spinning. The masked man. The sex. The blackouts. The syringe. He drugged me and now there's a fucking *present* on my counter and I don't know if I'm supposed to be terrified or—

I yank the ribbon off. The box opens with a soft creak. Not a ring.

An SD card. Black. Tiny.

And a folded piece of paper underneath it.

I unfold the note with numb fingers.

Three words in dark handwriting:

You earned it.

The SD card slides into my laptop with a quiet click.

I'm kneeling inside the tent. Fairy lights glowing above me. My hands won't stop shaking.

The folder opens automatically.

Twenty-seven video files.

I double-click the first one.

The footage starts. My apartment. Two days ago. I'm sitting on the floor. Wearing Daddy's hoodie. Hair in a messy bun. Writing. The timestamp says December 23rd, 4:47 PM.

The angle is from above. Hidden camera. He was watching me before the auction invitation even came.

I should close the laptop. I should throw the SD card in the trash and call the police and—

I keep watching.

The footage jumps forward. Time-lapse. Me reading the eviction notice. Me staring at the auction invitation.

He recorded all of it.

I click through all the videos. The limo, the preparation suite. The attendants washing me. Their hands on my body.

I'm holding my breath.

The auction. Me standing naked on the stage while men bid on me.

The cabin. The exam table. His hands. His mouth. His cock. Me coming so hard I blacked out.

I should stop.

But I don't.

The footage continues.

I click the fourteenth file.

The timestamp says December 24th, 11:32 PM. Six hours

after I blacked out the first time. The basement dungeon—if dungeons have floor-to-ceiling windows that overlook a perfect winter woods. Different angle. Wide shot capturing the entire space.

I'm bent over a padded bench. Wrists cuffed to the legs. Ankles spread and locked to a bar.

He's behind me. Naked except for the mask. His hard cock hovering and bouncing in the air as his hand comes down hard across my ass.

CRACK.

The sound makes me flinch even through the laptop speakers.

My body on screen arches. My mouth opens. But I don't scream.

I moan.

He spanks me again. And again. Rhythmic. Precise. My ass turning pink, then red.

Now that I'm watching this, I can feel those handprints.

He pauses. Runs his hand over the heated skin. Then reaches between my legs.

I watch myself grind back against his fingers.

No. No, I wouldn't—

But I am.

I'm watching myself do it.

He pulls his hand away. Brings it down again. Harder this time.

I come.

Right there. Just from the spanking. My whole body shaking against the bench, thighs trembling.

I fast forward… I'm on my back now. On that same exam table. But my legs aren't in stirrups. They're pulled up over my head. Ankles cuffed together above me. Completely exposed.

He's fucking me. Hard. One hand gripping my thigh, the other working a vibrator against my clit.

I'm screaming.

Not in pain.

In pleasure.

My voice is wrecked. Desperate. Begging. *"Please please please don't stop don't stop—"*

He doesn't stop.

I black out on camera. My body goes limp.

He pulls out. Sets the vibrator aside. Releases each restraint, calm, methodical. Then he lifts me and carries me over to the couch. He sits, me in his lap, and kisses my head, smoothing hair out of my eyes, whispering things I can't hear. But I know he's talking to me, I can see his lips moving.

Thirty seconds later on the timestamp, I wake up. I watch myself blink. Look around. Find his face. And then I reach for him.

I reach for *him*.

I scramble up, put myself in his lap. Kiss him. Grind against the erection still wet from being inside me.

The video ends, I put in the next one. I'm tied to a St. Andrew's cross. Arms and legs spread wide. He's using a flogger on my breasts. Soft strikes that make my nipples hard. Then he's on his knees. Mouth between my legs. Eating me out while I writhe against the restraints.

I come again. Blackout.

And again. Blackout.

And again. Blackout.

I stop counting after five.

Next video. I'm riding him. Bouncing on his cock like I'm possessed. His hands on my hips, guiding me, but I'm the one setting the pace.

Frantic. Desperate.

I look *happy*.

My face in the video is flushed. Eyes closed. Mouth open. Lost in it.

I don't look scared.

I look free.

What the fuck is wrong with me?

I fast forward. I'm on my stomach. Face down on the bondage table. Ass in the air. He's fucking me from behind while working a dildo into my ass at the same time.

I watch myself come so hard I scream into the padding.

Black out.

Wake up.

He's holding me. Whispering something I can't hear.

I nuzzle into his chest.

Stop it. Stop doing that.

Next video… he's using a wand vibrator on me while I'm strapped to a chair. My thighs are shaking so hard the whole chair rattles.

I'm begging him to stop.

But my hips are tilting up. Chasing the sensation.

He makes me come three times in a row without moving the vibrator away.

I black out.

Fast forward. I'm on top again. This time facing away from him. Reverse cowgirl. His hands are on my hips but I'm doing all the work. Riding him like my life depends on it. My hand between my legs. Rubbing my clit.

I come.

He comes.

I collapse forward onto his legs, panting.

Blackout.

The video jumps ahead.

Spanking bench again. But this time he's using a paddle. The heavy kind. Leather.

My ass is already red from before.

He brings it down.

I count the strikes in the video.

Twenty.

Thirty.

Forty.

I'm crying by the end. But when he stops and runs his fingers through my dripping pussy, I push back against his hand.

Begging for more.

He fucks me right there. Still bent over the bench. Hands gripping my bruised ass.

I scream when I come.

Another blackout.

I've lost count of how many times I came. How many times I blacked out. How many times he was there, holding me, or petting me, or kissing me when I came back.

The second-to-last file.

My hand hovers over the trackpad.

I don't want to see this.

But I click it anyway.

The timestamp says December 25th, 6:47 AM.

Back on the couch.

The mask is still on and I'm fucking him slow in his lap. Like... *slow* slow. Like not fucking, but lovemaking.

He's pulling my hair, my neck stretches back, his other hand goes to my throat—ah ha!

There!

He choked me!

But... he doesn't choke me. I put my hand on his, asking him to choke me. He refuses. Instead he plays with my clit until I black out again.

He comes too, groaning and grinding against me. Then he leans back, absently playing with my hair, breathing hard...

My eyes fly open. Panic. Running. Outside. Snow. Syringe.

Then—he carries me inside. Not rough. Gentle.

He lays me on a couch. Wraps a blanket around me.

The camera angle changes. Different room. My apartment.

He's here. In my apartment. Carrying my unconscious

body through the door and in to the bathroom. He undresses me.

I watch him peel off the clothes I was wearing—which aren't even mine. I went to his house naked. So these are his clothes.

I crawl out of the fort, walk into the bathroom, and sure enough—the clothes are on the floor. Black sweats and a black t-shirt with a Harvard logo on it, all faded and cracked.

This is real.

This really happened.

I go back into the fort and find the masked man lowering me into my own bathtub. I'm not unconscious, but clearly out of it as he washes my hair.

His hands work shampoo through the strands. Rinses it clean. Conditioner next. He's gentle. So fucking gentle.

He washes my face with a cloth. My neck. My shoulders.

When he lifts me out and dries me off, he's still careful. Holding me up as I wobble in place. Patting the towel against my skin with a gentle firmness.

Then he carries me back to the bed and lays me down. My bed, my clean bed inside my clean apartment.

He had it cleaned while I was at his house. He had it decorated with a tree and all the ornaments I lusted over for months. He put out a plate of cookies and milk. Had a child's glamping tent delivered so I could have a nice fort to live in while I write.

Who the fuck is this masked man?

He disappears off-screen.

When he comes back, he's holding clean clothes. My leggings. My sweatshirt.

Dressing me.

Pulling the leggings up my legs. Sliding the sweatshirt over my head. Positioning my arms through the sleeves.

He tucks me in. Pulls the blanket up to my chin. Smooths my hair back from my forehead. Then he leans down. Kisses the top of my head. His lips linger there for a moment. He says something. I can't hear it. The audio is muted or too quiet or—

I rewind. Turn the volume all the way up. Still can't hear it.

He straightens. Walks to the kitchen. The camera follows him. He picks up the cookie from the plate. Takes a bite. Sets it back down.

Then he leaves.

The footage ends.

I'm staring at the black screen.

My face is wet.

I don't know when I started crying again.

The last file is not sex. I knew that since I just watched the masked man tuck me in. But I wasn't expecting it to be *him*. Still wearing the mask, but looking very happy underneath it. He's smiling I can tell.

The timestamp says December 25th, 9:23 AM. So just a few hours ago.

"Hi, Scarletta." His voice is soft. Not the commanding tone from the basement fuck fest. Just... him. "I'm guessing you've watched the other files by now. I'm guessing you're freaking out about the blackouts."

Yes.

"I need you to understand something. What happened to you—it's called subspace psychosis." He pauses. Holds up a hand. "Not actual psychosis. That's just what subs call it. It's not dangerous. It's not a medical emergency."

I lean closer to the screen.

"It's a condition where subs who are deep bonded to their dominants enter a particular kind of subspace that affects memory formation. The blackouts weren't breathing problems. They weren't from blood pressure drops. It was your mind resetting because of the intensity of the orgasms combined with your neurological response to submission."

No.

"I know you don't believe me." He shifts forward. "Look up Dr. Alicia Friedman's research on altered states in BDSM relationships. Published 2019 in the Journal of Sexual Medicine. Look up the Kinsey Institute's study on subspace amnesia from 2021. It's real, Scarletta. It's documented."

He's lying. He has to be lying.

But I'm already opening a new tab. Typing the first citation. The article loads. Real. Peer-reviewed. Published in an actual medical journal.

Fuck.

I go back to the video.

He's quiet for a moment. Then he takes a breath. "But that's not why I'm recording this." Something in his tone shifts. Colder. "Clearly, you're having doubts about me. About this. About what happened."

Yes.

"And that's okay. You should. You barely know me. I drugged you to keep you calm after you woke up the last time. I've been stalking you for six months. I killed your ex-boyfriend. Your auction was fake, all the auctions are fake. It's a service I provide to men like me around the world."

Men like *him*?

I drugged you.

I killed your ex boyfriend.

I'm stalking you.

He says all this so calmly. Like he's listing groceries instead of felonies.

"So I'm going to leave you alone."

What?

"I'm going to give you space. Time. Whatever you need.

The money's in your account—you can check. You don't owe me anything, Scarletta. The contract's fulfilled. You earned every penny."

I pause the video. Because I don't know what I'm feeling right now. What the fuck am I feeling right now?

Did I have a good time?

Well. I'm alive. That's something. He didn't kill me. He could have. He killed Derek. Cut off his fingers. Mutilated him. Burned the body.

But he didn't kill me.

He fucked me unconscious, drugged me, and then he *tucked me in.*

I liked it.

I liked it.

I shouldn't have liked it. Normal girls don't like that. Normal girls don't get off on being bought, and used, and drugged, and discarded.

"There are cameras in your apartment, Scarletta."

I blow out a breath, completely overwhelmed.

"I left a document on your lap top called my_eyes.docx. It's saved to your desktop. It shows where they all are and how to turn them off via the app I use to spy on you."

This is so fucked up.

"There's another doc called her_thoughts.docx on the desktop," he says. "It's got the log in details for the keystroke recording hack I used to spy on your writing. I've left instructions on how to turn it off." He smiles at me. Or... the camera, whatever. "It was fun. I'm glad you got what you needed. Thank you for giving me what I needed back. As I said, the money's in your account. I hope you have an amazing life."

Then... he reaches forward and stops the recording.

And that's it, I guess.

It's over.

EPILOGUE - CALEB

Blood for Blood hammers through the speakers as I turn down the long driveway to my log mansion. Same song. Same ritual. Different body.

Tall firs and pines press in from both sides, snow-heavy branches creating a tunnel of white and shadow. My hands are steady on the wheel, not even a hint of shaking after the adrenaline rush. Just the familiar hum of satisfaction that settles in after I balance the scales.

The barn appears through the trees. I pull the Jeep inside, kill the engine, and enjoy the way the silence drops like a curtain.

My clothes are soaked through with blood. Not my blood, it's never my blood. I peel off the thermal shirt, the jeans, the boots. The furnace fire roars to life when I open the grate and toss it all in. I watch the fabric catch, curl, then blacken. The smoke disappearing through the chimney vent.

Evidence erased.

The cold hits me the second I step outside. Naked. Minus fifteen according to the thermometer mounted on the barn wall. Snow crunches under my bare feet as my breath spews out in front of me in long, white clouds.

I don't feel the cold. Not really. It's just data. Temperature. Wind chill. Irrelevant.

Steam rises from the surface of the hot tub in thick coils. I climb in and sink down to my shoulders. The water stings every inch of exposed skin. I close my eyes. Let the heat dissolve the blood residue, the gun oil, the smell of fear and piss from the warehouse.

He earned it. They always do.

I replay a little of it, but mostly I'm thinking about *her*.

I'm always thinking about her.

So I get out and walk back inside through the mudroom. My cock is half-hard from the temperature shift. I ignore it. Shower in the master bath using the handheld to blast away anything the hot tub missed. Dry off, then pull on grey sweatpants and a black thermal henley.

Downstairs I grab a whiskey and my laptop and hit the couch. The screen glows to life when I open it—sixteen camera feeds load automatically.

Scarletta sits cross-legged inside the glamping tent I set up, laptop balanced on her thighs, wearing my fucking clothes.

Black Harvard t-shirt. Black sweatpants. She wears them at least once a week.

Every time I see that shirt stretched across her tits, something tightens in my chest. Possession mixed with satisfaction. She's marked herself with me and doesn't even realize it. Or maybe she does.

I take a long pull of whiskey and set the glass down.

She never disabled the cameras. Never changed her passwords. Never followed a single instruction I gave her for removing the surveillance.

I discovered this three days after I dropped her off. Opened the feeds expecting static or black screens—evidence she'd yanked the hardware, wiped the software, reclaimed her privacy like any sane person would.

Instead I found her bent over her laptop in that tent, typing.

Wearing my shirt.

I pulled my cock out right then. Came all over my hand watching her existence continue like I hadn't just fucked her unconscious, drugged her, and confessed to murder.

It's been seven weeks. She hasn't touched the cameras once. Hasn't even tried to disable the keystroke hack. Hasn't even changed her fucking bank account password.

I don't understand it. Pleased, yes. Intrigued, absolutely. Aroused every single night when I load these feeds and watch her pretend I'm not watching.

But what's her motive?

Does she want me to keep watching? Is this permission without words? Or is she performing now, aware of the audience, giving me a show?

She's different than she was before the auction. Cleaner. Her hair's shorter—professional cut, layered around her face. New clothes that actually fit instead of drowning her. I've seen her paint her nails twice. Makeup appears some days, subtle but present.

Still writes, but the frantic pace is gone. Before, she'd lose herself for six, eight, ten hours straight. Emerge only to piss, or shove food in her mouth, or fuck herself with her fingers before diving back in.

Now she writes in controlled bursts. Two hours, break. Three hours, break.

The masturbation frequency dropped too. Used to be four, five, six times a day.

Now it's once. Maybe twice if she's working on a particularly filthy scene.

But the last few days, something shifted.

She's writing faster again. Stops every twenty minutes to slip her hand beneath the waistband of my sweatpants.

Sometimes she stares directly into the camera mounted in

the tent's corner. Holds eye contact with the lens while she rubs her clit. Mouths words I can't hear because this feed has no audio.

Sometimes she closes her eyes and pretends I'm not there at all.

The Watcher.

Her Watcher.

I slip my hand into my sweats and pull my cock free. Already hard. Already leaking.

On screen, Scarletta's fingers pause mid-keystroke, hovering over her laptop's keyboard for just a moment before her hand abandons the keys entirely. She shifts in the camping chair—that restless, telltale squirm I've come to recognize—and slides her palm beneath the soft black cotton of my Harvard shirt.

The fabric bunches and lifts as her hand travels upward. I can't see the exact moment her fingers find her nipple through the camera's angle. Can't watch her pinch it, can't observe whether she uses her thumb and forefinger or just rolls it beneath her palm.

But I know.

I know because her head tips back slightly. Because her lips part on an exhale I can't hear but can imagine perfectly— that soft, surprised sound she makes when sensation spikes through her body.

Because her free hand grips the armrest of the camping chair, knuckles whitening as she braces herself against whatever she's doing to her own breast beneath my shirt.

I wrap my fingers more firmly around my shaft, adjusting my grip with practiced precision, and stroke myself with slow, deliberate pulls as her other hand disappears into her sweats.

My sweats.

My rhythm matches the restless shifting of her body on screen—each subtle movement of her hips translating directly to the tightening pressure of my fist. My thumb swipes across the head, spreading the bead of moisture gathering there, and I suppress the urge to speed up.

Control. Always control.

But fuck, she makes it difficult when she touches herself like this—when she forgets the camera exists and surrenders completely to whatever fantasy is playing out behind those closed eyelids.

I zoom in on the laptop screen visible over her shoulder in the feed. The keystroke logger runs separate from the camera feeds—background process she still hasn't detected—but I prefer watching her type in real time when the camera angle cooperates.

The document title sits at the top of her screen.

The Watcher - Chapter 11

My cock jumps in my hand.

She's been working on this for weeks. I've watched the word count climb—twelve thousand, fifteen thousand, twenty-three thousand. Currently sitting at thirty-one thousand, four hundred and seventy-two words.

Not published. Not posted to DarkDesires. Saved locally in a folder labeled "Private - DO NOT UPLOAD."

I read every word the moment she types it.

The Watcher is about a man who surveils a woman through hidden cameras. Studies her routines. Learns her patterns. Breaks into her apartment to touch her things, smell her clothes, read her writing.

The Watcher orchestrates situations. Creates problems. Offers himself as the solution.

The Watcher eventually takes her. Keeps her. Makes her understand she was always meant to belong to him.

It's about me.

It's about us.

She hasn't changed a single detail except the names. The protagonist is "Violet." The stalker is "James."

James has cameras in Violet's apartment. James hacked her laptop. James read all her stories before she published them. James killed her abusive ex-boyfriend with his bare hands.

James tattooed Violet's face across his entire torso before they ever met.

Every scene I recognize. Every confession she puts in Violet's mouth is something Scarletta said to me in that playroom. Every dark fantasy James enacts is something I did to her on that exam table, in those restraints, with my fingers buried inside her pussy.

She's writing our story. Fictionalizing it just enough to publish eventually, maybe. Or maybe this one stays private forever—her way of processing what happened between us.

Her way of telling me she understood exactly what I was doing and wanted it anyway.

On DarkDesires, her readers are losing their minds.

ScarletSins where are you???

It's been 7 weeks since "Confession" posted. Are you okay??

Did something happen to her? Should we be worried?

She always posts at least once a week. This isn't like her.

I've been monitoring the forum obsessively. Watching strangers worry about her disappearance. Watching them speculate.

One commenter—username DevotedReader88—posts every single day asking if anyone's heard from her.

I know it's not actually concern. It's entitlement. They want their content. Their free emotional labor. Their parasocial connection to a woman whose real name they don't even know.

But Scarletta isn't writing for them anymore.

She's writing for me.

Her bank account tells a different story than the woman on screen touching herself in my clothes.

I pull up the monitoring software tracking her finances.

Chase checking account ending in 4738. Current balance: $6,247.83.

Seven weeks ago, on December 26th, the day after I dropped her off, the balance read $45,047.32.

She burned through thirty-nine thousand dollars in less than two months.

Not shopping sprees. Not vacations. Not the kind of frivolous spending you'd expect from someone who just made more money than she'd ever seen.

She paid her landlord first—one lump sum clearing four months of back rent plus three months forward. Then the utility companies that had sent final notices. Internet, power, water. The parking tickets that had threatened collections. The two maxed-out credit cards that had been accruing interest at twenty-three percent—she paid them to zero and then immediately cut them up.

The student loans got a massive payment. Not enough to kill them entirely, but enough to move her out of default status. Enough to stop the threatening letters. The car payment—she'd been two months behind—caught up and pushed ahead by one.

The rest leaked away in small amounts. Coffee shops. Gas. Groceries. Normal human expenses for someone who'd been operating on empty for months.

She paid off everything she could.

Responsible. Practical. Deeply fucking depressing.

This wasn't "fun money." This was damage control. Financial triage.

She climbed out of the hole just enough to see daylight but not enough to actually stand upright. Still underground. Still surviving, not living.

Still no job.

The copywriting gigs she ignored before Christmas are gone completely now. Fiverr account deactivated due to too many missed deadlines. Upwork profile sits abandoned with a 2.1-star rating and angry client reviews.

"Never delivered final draft. Stopped responding to messages."

"Wasted my time. DO NOT HIRE."

She hasn't applied for new work. Hasn't updated her portfolio. Hasn't done anything except write The Watcher and touch herself in my shirt.

She doesn't seem to care.

This is the part that bothers me.

On screen, her hand moves faster beneath the sweatpants. Her back arches slightly off the camping chair. Her laptop slides to the side, forgotten, as both hands disappear into the fabric.

My cock throbs in my fist. I stroke harder, faster, precome slicking my palm as I time my rhythm to match the restless grinding of her hips.

She's close. I can see it in the way her thighs tremble. The way her free hand grips the armrest of that ridiculous camping chair hard enough to leave marks.

I reach for my laptop with my left hand, cock still gripped tight in my right, and pull up the custom interface I built three months ago.

One button. Red. Labeled simply: SEND.

My thumb hovers over the trackpad.

On screen, Scarletta's head falls back. Her mouth opens on what I know is a moan I can't hear. Her hand moves frantically between her legs, chasing release.

I click.

Her laptop dings. Can't hear it, but I know it does because Scarletta's eyes snap open. Her hand freezes mid-stroke. She stares at her screen for three full seconds, chest heaving, thighs still spread, fingers probably still touching her clit beneath my sweatpants.

Deciding.

She pulls her hand free and reaches for the laptop instead.

Good girl.

My cock jumps as I watch her open the message. Watch her read.

SUBJECT: EXCLUSIVE INVITATION -
Valentine's Day Scavenger Hunt

Dear ScarletSins,

Your performance at the Triple XMas Auction exceeded all expectations. Based on client feedback and documented excellence, you've been selected for our most exclusive event.

Would you like to hunt for the ultimate Valentine's prize?

The Valentine's Day Scavenger Hunt connects our highest-rated participants with curated challenges designed to test limits, reward bravery, and deliver compensation beyond standard contracts.

Event Details:

Duration: 48 hours (February 14th, 12:00 PM - February 16th, 12:00 PM)

Format: Individual scavenger hunt with progressive challenges

Objective: Collect all pieces. Complete the hunt. Claim your prize.

Base Compensation: $50,000

Make this Valentine's unforgettable—for yourself AND for someone who values exactly what you offer.

> Interested? Click below to confirm
> attendance and review terms.
>
> [CONFIRM INTEREST]

I snicker. Actually laugh out loud in the empty room.

Scavenger hunt. She has no fucking idea what I've planned for this one.

On screen, Scarletta's cursor hovers over the button. Just hovers there, trembling slightly—or maybe that's her hand shaking.

She bites her bottom lip.

My hand moves faster on my shaft. Grip tightening. Control slipping just enough to make this dangerous.

Her thighs are still spread. Her other hand drifts back down to the waistband of my sweatpants like she can't help herself.

She's going to touch herself while she decides whether to click.

Fuck.

My hips lift off the couch. Precome drips down my knuckles. I don't bother wiping it away.

Her finger twitches on the trackpad.

Click it. *Fucking click it.*

The cursor moves. Settles directly over [CONFIRM INTEREST].

Hovers.

I hold my breath.

She clicks.

My orgasm rips through me so hard I see white. Come shoots across my stomach, my chest, my hand still working my cock through every violent pulse as I watch her screen load the confirmation page.

RESERVATION CONFIRMED.

Participant 847-SK-2847 locked for
Valentine's Day Scavenger Hunt.

Pickup: Right now.

I collapse back against the couch, cock still twitching in my fist, and watch her stare at her screen.

Then she finds the camera inside the glamping fort. Her eyes lock onto the lens, and for one suspended heartbeat, she just stares.

She knows I'm watching.

I'm *always* watching.

Her lips part. Slowly. Deliberately. She brings her hand to her mouth—the same hand that was between her thighs moments ago—and slides two fingers past her lips. Her eyes never leave the camera. Never leave *me*.

She sucks them into her mouth. Slow. Thorough. Cheeks hollowing as she drags them back out, glistening wet. Then pushes them back in. Deeper this time. Her throat works around them.

My cock jerks in my fist. Still sensitive. Still half-hard even after coming so violently.

She pulls her fingers free and holds them up to the camera. Wet. Obscene. Then she smiles—small, wicked, knowing— and mouths two words I can read perfectly on her lips.

Challenge accepted.

Jesus fucking Christ.

I reach for my phone with my clean hand, heart hammering against my ribs, and type the message I've been waiting seven weeks to send.

Pack a bag, my good little slut.

You're going on a trip.

CONTINUE THE STORY

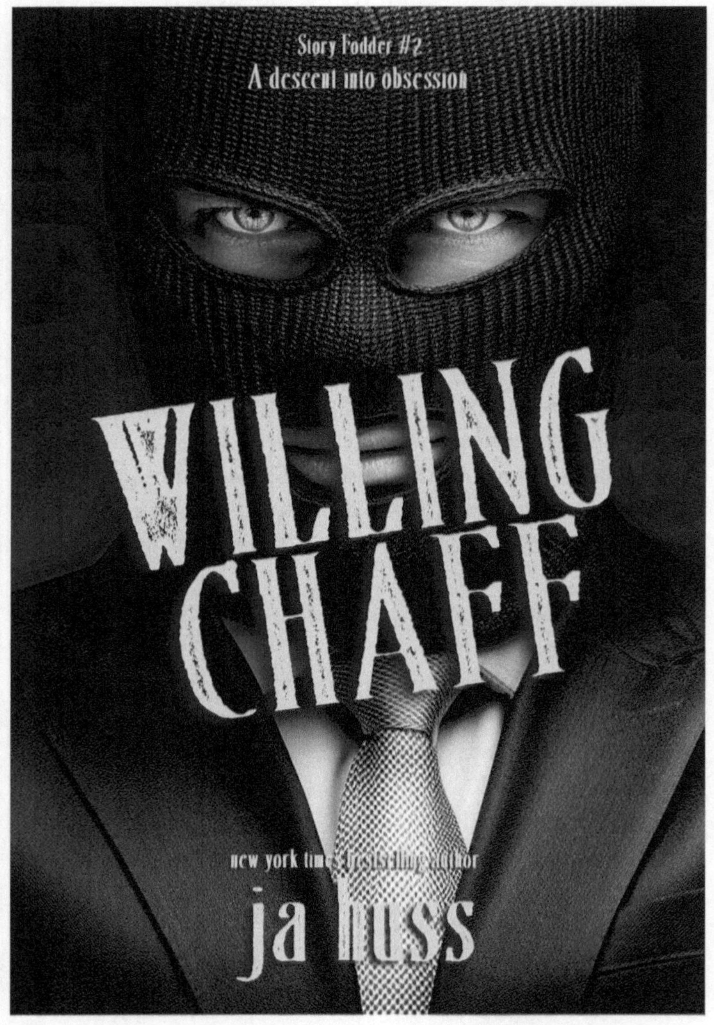

STORY FODDER #2 - WILLING CHAFF

48 Hours. No Limits. No Mercy. No Excuses.

ScarletSins

Check here if you agree to be hunted. Yes.

Check here if you agree to be caught. Hell yes.

I told myself the first time was desperation. The second time is just... follow-up. Fact-checking. Character development. Research.

Why am I doing this again?

Story fodder.

That's what I keep telling myself.

The auction starts in three hours and I've already checked the box I swore I wouldn't.

Run.

Watcher

Check here if you've been counting the days. Every single one.

Check here if you let her think this was her idea. Obviously.

She came back. Told herself it was for the writing. Told herself she's gathering material. She has no idea what I'm gathering.

Why am I doing this?

Because watching isn't enough anymore.

The auction starts in three hours and the hunt is already over.

She just hasn't stopped running yet.

———

This book contains: a man who should be in prison, a woman who should know better, and scenes that will make you google "is this okay?" (It's not. Enjoy.)

———

Vibe warnings:

👁️🖥️🖤 He's always watching
🔪⚖️💀 Serial Killer with a Code
🛏️😢📓 Your therapist will have questions
🚩⛓️🖤 Trust issues are justified
👻🔥💀 Sorry not sorry
🏃⛓️💀 She runs. Not fast enough
🐺👁️🔥 Prey/predator dynamics
👉💀⚔️ Touch her and find out
🔒✅ Safe words are used
⛓️💔🖤 Trauma bonding
🔪💀🩸 Murd3r & Tortvr3

END OF BOOK SHIT

END OF BOOK SHIT

Welcome to the End of Book Shit. This is the part of the book where I get to say anything I want about the story you just read. It's never edited, excuse my typos. I'm on Day 7 of the 12 Days of Giveaways and… yeah. To say that I'm running on fumes would be generous.

———

This story is… something.

You just read a book about a stalker billionaire who rigged a fake sex auction to claim an erotica writer he's been watching for six months.

And you're still here.

That says something about both of us.

I get it. It's… um… yeah. It's that. But sometimes you just need to write the unhinged thing, ya know? The one where he has her face tattooed on his body before they ever meet. The one where she's an erotica writer and he's read every single story and decided to make them real. The one with the Bic pen scene that came from... actually, I don't know where that came from. The same place in my brain that thought butter

235

was the perfect substitute for anal lube, probably. (Lol I totally riffed off the butter scene in Mr. Perfect for the Bic pen.)

I've been writing dark romance since 2013. Over a hundred books across two names. I've hit #3 in the entire Kindle store. I've also taken years off to breathe. This industry will eat you alive if you let it, and I've watched it happen to people I love.

So I don't let it.

Triple Xmas exists because I wanted to write something fun. Something that didn't take itself too seriously while still delivering the goods. The meta-narrative thing—the erotica writer whose fantasies become real—that wasn't an accident. I've spent over a decade writing about dark desires, taboo scenarios, the things people crave but won't say out loud. And I've watched readers find those books and feel seen. Feel less broken. Feel like maybe their fantasies don't make them monsters.

That's Scarletta's arc.

That's probably why you're here.

I wrote Triple Xmas in the end of what I'll generously call "my lost year"—which was actually selling my ranch, moving out of state, RV-ing with my dogs across Wyoming, Nebraska, Kansas, South Dakota, Iowa, Missouri, and Arkansas. I was looking for a new house. I put in FIVE offers before this one went through. It was kinda weird. But, like most things in life —it just works out the way it was meant to.

It did mean that I had no time to release books. I did have time to write books—mostly before I sold my ranch and then after I bought this house. But releasing books is another animal. Writing is relaxing. It's 'the thing I do everyday.'

Releasing is never fun for me. It's not the marketing, either. I actually like marketing.

So I wrote a whole bunch of books and never released them.

I wrote this one last minute. I had that little panic attack that writers get–the one that says people forgot about me. They're never gonna remember me…

So I decided to whip up a dark Christmas story. But only because the idea came to me over the summer and it was pretty basic as far as JA Huss plots go.

Welcome to the Christmas Eve Sex Auction.

But a funny thing happened on the way to publishing this story… I got more ideas. That little fuckin' muse showed up in my head telling me to pull a thread here, a string there… and before I knew it, I had a six-book series on my hands.

Now, I do have the second book up for pre-order and you can get it here, but these are standalones. There's not gonna be a cliff—except for the next book set up-if there is one, which is not a cliff, it's a teaser.

If you're finding me for the first time: hi. I have a lot of books. A lot. Two names, multiple subgenres, over a decade of accumulated chaos. My website is jahuss.com. Every December I do the 12 Days of Giveaways, which I've been running in various forms for over ten years. If you're reading this in December 2025, that's probably happening right now and I'm working 16-hour days trying to keep my shit together.

If you've been with me for a while: thank you. Genuinely. I know I took most of 2025 off to move, and regroup, and remember who I am outside of release schedules. The fact that you're still here, still reading, still showing up—that's not nothing.

That's *everything*.

I see you.
I appreciate you.
I love you.

What's coming:
My 2026 is already insane. I've got a shit-ton of stuff coming. ALL the books I wrote in 2025 but didn't release. Plus some new shit too—like this little fun project you just read.
It's a lot, people.
So get ready.

One more thing:
If you see yourself in Scarletta—in her shame spirals, her blanket forts, her desperate need to be truly seen by someone who won't flinch — you're not broken.
You're perfect just the way you are.

Thank you for reading, thank you for reviewing, and see you in the next book.

Julie
JA Huss
December 7, 2025

ABOUT THE AUTHOR

JA Huss is a scientist, New York Times and USA Today bestselling author. Her self-published romantasy Sparktopia was named an Audible Editors' Best of the Year selection in 2024, and several of her audiobooks have been nominated for the Audie and SOVA Awards. A 2019 RITA finalist, Huss has had five books optioned for film and television and co-wrote a television pilot for MGM with actor and screenwriter Jonathan McClain.